A Deep Purple Hue

Book One of the Gordan Hudde Series

MARK HUDSON

ALSO BY MARK HUDSON

"If the broad light of day could be let in upon men's actions, it would purify them as the sun disinfects."
- Louis Brandeis.

CONTENTS

1

Gordan Hudde's eyelids began to flutter as he regained consciousness. It was nearly the same feeling people have when they realize they have been dreaming during an afternoon nap. It took a moment for him to recover and Hudde tried to keep his eyes closed while he came back to his senses. He mentally conducted a check for injuries, then realized he was being dragged unceremoniously by his right ankle by a man he had earlier nicknamed "Igor."

The last time he had been knocked unconscious was his first jump years ago in airborne school. He had executed something commonly called a "three-point landing," meaning the body parts that struck the earth came in this painful order: heels, ass, and head. That day, he had sprung back to his senses very quickly, collected his chute, and checked in before he could be identified for additional training or, worse yet, sent back to a remedial week of training with another class, further behind.

This time was much worse. He had been attempting to sneak into a dilapidated, small building deep in the war-torn area in Latakia, Syria.

Hudde allowed his head to roll to the left as it bumped along the hard-packed dirt floor. He saw a large dog-kennel-type cage with a hooded and hog-tied occupant. The prisoner rolled to his side, attempting to listen to whatever was happening with Hudde, and that sign of life was a very welcome one.

Now Hudde peeked up to look at Igor, a tall, heavy man, who was holding Hudde's ankle with his right hand and dragging Hudde's rucksack with the other. Hudde could make out his handgun and K-bar knife sticking out of Igor's belt at the center of his wide back.

It appeared that their ultimate destination was the front of the nearly empty building, a small wood-and-glass enclosed office built around the front door of the place. This was not the hasty plan Hudde had created to free the prisoner, and the last place he wanted to be was anywhere near the front door.

He made some noise to announce he was awake and began to squirm gently, pulling both of his knees toward his chest.

Igor dropped the American's bag and stopped to grab both ankles, pulling him the last few feet into the office where his friend waited in the only chair. That friend, christened "Laurel" by Hudde earlier, was now rising to his feet to see what was being dragged in.

As Hudde struggled, he noticed Laurel reaching under the flap to his WWII-style holster. Hudde shoved both his feet as hard as he could into the big man's sternum, sending him stumbling the last couple of steps backward until he caught a heel on the one step into the office, falling into the knees of Laurel, who stood in the door.

Laurel fell backward and Hudde heard him slam into the wooden front door with a thud. He took this time to scramble and slide to a stop at the side of the metal cage.

"Dick Tracy — is that you?" Hudde asked.

"Hooyah, mother fucker!" was the reply. The captive's energy and attitude brought a brief smile from Hudde.

"One mike" (one minute). Hudde rolled back to look at the noise behind him. Laurel had extracted himself from Igor and cleared his weapon from the leather holster. Standing back in the doorway, he leveled the small barrel in their general direction.

Hudde silently prayed that the guy was a lousy shot, but just then, a previous prayer was answered when three pounds of *Semtex* exploded from just outside the front door, sending pieces of Igor and Laurel's better half — Hudde called him "Hardy" — inward. Laurel flew forward, landing face first in the dirt Hudde had just been dragged across.

Taking advantage of the carnage, Hudde jumped up before the pieces of wood, glass, and jihadi started hitting the floor. He rolled Laurel onto his back and stomped his throat three times. He found his K-bar and used it to cut the throat of the still-alive-but-injured Igor. There was no need to look for Hardy — he was dead before the blast.

Hudde couldn't find his handgun in the mess.

He ran back and dropped back down to the cage; only a small metal S-hook was threaded through the hasp. Hudde guessed that they had not been too worried about any rescue attempt.

Hudde dragged Navy SEAL Jim Foster from inside the cage and cut him free.

"Can you run?" he asked the SEAL.

"And fight!" Foster added.

"Good — let's get the fuck outta here!" Hudde picked up his smoking rucksack on the way to the back door.

■ ■ ■

Eighteen Hours Earlier:

CIA agent Gordan Hudde was shuffling through the dusty streets of Latakia, looking for a contact. His head was covered in the traditional turban of the Tuareg tradition to help him blend in. A poncho covered his shoulders as well as the heavy, worn-out canvas rucksack he carried. Hudde walked past the area where he was supposed to meet his contact and then walked slowly in concentric circles, making sure he was not being followed and hopefully lessening the chances that he would walk into a trap.

His contact was one Fuhad Musa, who was unknown by any of the world's intelligence agencies when they had run his name. Given the state of the region right now, this was to be expected — but this was no time for Hudde to relax.

At the meeting, just inside a small storefront, Musa offered him tea. Musa had brought two men with him, and they were sitting at the table just behind them.

"You were supposed to come alone," Hudde rasped.

Musa turned to look at the men behind him. "They hate the Tigers of Islam; you do not need to worry."

"So you can tell me where they're holed up?" Hudde placed a small map on the table.

Musa pushed the map away. "No — you must not be so obvious! Please meet me back here at nine o'clock tomorrow night, and we shall show you." Dark gaps and gums showed between his yellow teeth when he smiled.

Gordan picked up the glass and allowed the liquid to touch his lips, but he did not drink; he noticed that Musa had not, either.

Hudde pulled down on his Spartan-looking black beard to ponder. "No. I think you better show me on the map."

Musa turned and spoke to his compatriots. Hudde would later swear that one of them was Russian.

"No. This we cannot do. We must show you ourselves tomorrow night." Musa was all in on this; he folded his arms across his chest to signal that this was his final offer.

Hudde knew what the answer was going to be but pulled on his beard some more before nodding. "Okay. 2300 hours tomorrow."

"Yes, yes."

Hudde nodded, pulled his *shemagh* back up over his face, and walked back out into the quickly diminishing daylight. He lost the tail after twenty minutes and walked down a tight alley in a shopping district that had no real traffic.

The shop on the left appeared to be empty, and he was able to swing up onto the roof after leaping onto an overhang near a locked back door. There was a tarp covering some artillery holes on the back corner of the roof. It probably kept out very little when it rained, but it might do well enough to keep out sun and dust. Hudde slid under it and felt protected from any prying eyes; hell, he might even get some sleep.

Before he drifted off to sleep, he wondered what his next move was going to be. He knew he was not going to the meeting tomorrow night. Maybe he should try to tail them when they left the meeting without him. Was this operation something the Russians were running, or were they just tagging along, trying to figure out what the Americans were up to? Had they absorbed this newer terrorist organization, or was it a part of what was left of the Syrian government?

"Fuck it," Hudde whispered and drifted off to sleep.

He awoke to the roar of an unmufflered Toyota pickup. Hudde peeked through the cracked façade of the roof to see it slide to a stop at the rear of a similar building just across the back alley. A 20-millimeter anti-aircraft gun was bolted into the bed of the truck. Hudde turned his wrist over to see that it was just after 2200 hours.

Hudde cursed his luck and prayed they weren't about to open fire and ruin his chances of getting some additional shuteye.

The guy in the back of the truck jumped out and pulled a chain from the long, low door that ran on rollers on an overhead track above. He pushed the door and it screamed in protest. It would have woken Hudde if the truck hadn't already done that.

A Mercedes 280 CE barreled too fast down the alley and nearly slammed into the pickup as it slid to a stop, throwing up a cloud of dust that drifted off on the breeze. Three doors opened, and three men got out, surrounding the unopened door. One of the men pulled opened the door, and then the biggest guy in the group — it was "Igor" — yanked a man out onto the dirt. That man was hooded, with his hands tied behind him.

The captive rolled with the momentum and staggered to his feet. He was able to kick a man before he was thrown back down to the ground, but, in the scuffle, his hood had come off.

One of the men was holding a large curved blade under the captive's chin, while a skinny and dirty-looking man hogtied the prisoner. Hudde could see that it was "Laurel and Hardy." Hardy needlessly grabbed a handful of the captive's hair and pulled up, giving Hudde a perfect look at the man being held prisoner. Hudde had been in-country nearly a month now and was unaware that the coalition forces had lost a man. But it was still tough to watch this man's treatment, as Hudde had actually served with this operator and his team not too long ago. It was Jim Foster, an American Navy SEAL.

Gordan wiped the dust out of his eyes and stared into the darkness to double-check until his eyes began to water. Yes, this was one of our guys, and right now it was six tangos to one Gordan Hudde — not odds the Vegas guys would put much money on.

Gordan took a swig from his canteen and leaned back against the small wall to think. He pulled down on his beard as he thought.

His mission was crap right now, but by trying to follow the men the next night, Hudde thought that it still may have a chance for success.

The screeching wheels above the door signaled movement, and Gordan leaned back to see what was happening. Two of the men climbed into the Mercedes and drove off in a cloud of dust.

Now it was four to one. Gordan leaned back and reached down to a cargo pocket where he felt the silencer to his 9mm.

He heard the terrible screech of those rusty, dirty, and oil-less steel door wheels. He leaned back and watched as two more men climbed into the pickup and sped off.

Fuck. Decision made. No way he was leaving a man behind with odds at two to one.

He pushed the ruck up, over his shoulders, and then slid silently over the side of the building, dropping softly onto the dirt. He stood in the darkness and stared at the door the men had been coming and going from. He was confident it was not secured, but he would have to start shooting the moment he entered the room, as those rusty wheels were as good as an alarm system.

Hudde decided to risk walking up front. He couldn't remember if there were windows at the front door; there certainly were none along the side. He crossed the alley and silently crept to the front of the street; there was almost no traffic during the day, and at night, there were no pedestrians and no light. The only sound was the occasional jet aircraft flying low overhead, along with sporadic gunfire in the distance. Off on the horizon, the sky lit up momentarily, like the sun was rising; the thunder came after. Hudde couldn't help but wonder whose bombs were exploding. He crept along the front of the building toward a small overhang, where he knew a door was slightly recessed from the street. A few feet past the door was a small window. To formulate a decent plan of action, Hudde knew he had to get a look in that window.

Just as Hudde was about to cross in front of the door, he heard voices rise inside and the latch on the door rattled. Hudde flattened against the wall and waited. A wedge of light cascaded across the street, and a shadow entered the light. The guy Hudde had nick-named "Hardy" stepped into the street.

"Proving you know nothing!" Hardy yelled back into the room he was exiting.

Hardy reached back to pull the door closed, and the moment that darkness returned to the street, Hudde was upon him. The thin blade of his boot knife slid easily through the man's neck from artery to artery.

Hudde stopped the initial gasp with a gloved hand, and then there was no need, as the knife also cut the larynx. Hudde kept the dead body supported enough that it did not make a noise when it dropped to the ground.

Hudde wiped his knife on the dead man's shoulder and then slid it back into his boot. He was about to pull out his silencer and make a mad dash inside to take on whoever was left when he heard a car racing up the road.

Hudde dropped over the body and hoped that the occupants of the oncoming car were not paying attention.

The Mercedes returned down the alley.

Fuck! Who was that? Would the truck and the men return as well?

Hudde heard car doors slamming and the screech announcing the opening and closing of the rear door. He slid to the window and peeked over the sill; there was "Laurel" sitting right there! Hudde did not see how many more men had returned to upend his odds.

Hudde crawled back and opened his rucksack near "Hardy's" cooling body.

"I need you to do me a favor. Who knows? Maybe I can get you those seventy virgins posthumously," he whispered to the corpse.

Pulling three pounds of Semtex from his bag, he set it up with a two-minute digital fuse. He placed the explosives in the general long rectangular shape going up the door from the ground to a height of about two feet. Then he dragged Hardy to a seated position and gently allowed him to sit back against the explosives. This would allow a greater force to be blasted inward, hopefully giving Gordan a distraction to take advantage of.

Hudde patted the dead man on the head as he stood. "Thanks, man."

He now had two minutes to get to the back door and come in, guns blazing. Hudde wondered how many men were now inside as he came to the back corner and looked quickly around. He had heard the door open and close; he was thinking that two men were left in the Mercedes. So, maybe, two more had just returned. His odds might now be three against one.

The Mercedes was parked pointing at him, trunk open. Hudde was tempted to go around and look but didn't want to be out of position when his explosives went off. He drew his handgun just as he thought he heard the gravel crunch from behind him. He instinctively rolled his shoulders up and tried to get his head down just as it went dark.

■ ■ ■

Jim Foster was limping badly as they ran from the smoking, dusty ruin of the small warehouse. His left arm hung and swung at an odd angle, maybe broken; he obviously had been beaten soundly while being held. Hudde watched as the tall, lanky man winced as he folded himself into the Mercedes' passenger seat. Hudde threw his ruck into Foster's lap as he slid behind the wheel.

Hudde looked at Foster as he turned the key; the engine roared to life and they shot out of the alley and headed east into the country. Hudde went two intersections up and further inland before turning and making his way back toward the coast.

It was only a few miles, and they made it to a dock with two dozen smaller fishing and recreational types of small watercraft. Hudde took up his rucksack and pulled Foster back to his feet.

They found a fifteen-foot boat with a full tank of gas and two seats behind a small windscreen. A tiny forward area would allow one of them to get some sleep, out of sight, if the opportunity arose.

Gordan studied Foster. "Can you take us out to deep water?"

Foster didn't say anything; he just started casting off and getting the screws in the water.

Hudde sat on one of the seats and dug through the canvas bag. He came up with something like a heavy-duty pen. He twisted the two ends in opposite directions and depressed a heavy rubber button on one end. He turned the item over several times, looking at it.

Foster saw him. "What's that?"

"Calling for a ride…I hope. I was just thinking that they should put a small blinking light on it or something to let you know if it's working."

Hudde shrugged and dropped it into a cargo pocket.

"Where to?" Foster asked.

"I guess you can stop if we make it to Cyprus." Hudde smiled in the darkness.

"You want me to take over?"

"No."

Foster turned to look at him, keeping his right arm, the "good" one, lying over the wheel, keeping them traveling west out into the Mediterranean.

"Maybe you could answer a couple of questions."

Hudde nodded. "Sure, if I can."

"You know a fellow spook named Kincade?"

Hudde nodded. "I met him once — son of somebody important." Hudde paused, further studying Foster. "I didn't send him a Christmas card this year, if you're wondering."

Foster nodded in understanding. "Listen, Hudde. You've worked with us. Work your plan, and then ride up front with us. It gives the team confidence that you believe in the operation you've planned so much that you're willing to take on that risk."

"I have to..." Gordan started to say.

"That's just it — you don't, and he never did. He even got himself some local heavies to pull security for him."

Hudde nodded. "Okay. We all agree the guy was an asshole. I don't think he even is working with us anymore."

"Do you keep a deck of 'most wanted' cards?"

Hudde peeked over the windscreen. "No. Can't say I do. I know who most are."

"Farouq Mustafa..."

Hudde interrupted. "Jack of Spades."

"Yeah. We got word he was up in a small village north of Mosul, and they sent us to take a shot."

"Hey, Foster — maybe you shouldn't be sharing this. Maybe you're too beat up and tired. Maybe I'm not the guy who should be hearing this."

Foster shook his head. "Maybe you're exactly the person who should hear this. I'm not sure I'll include any of it in my debrief."

Hudde shrugged his shoulders. "Alright, then."

"Our team gets about twelve hundred yards out on a ridgeline overlooking this village; we're pretty well established and begin glassing. A helicopter comes in low over the north, and out of one of the mud huts comes our boy, the Jack of Spades."

"Did you guys get a shot off?"

"No. I had the binos and had an unobstructed view. Can you guess who's with him? That's right — Mr. Kinkade walked out into this field to meet the chopper. The chopper was Iranian, Hudde, complete with all the markings."

"What?"

"Oh, it gets better. Once it touches down, out pops Victor Crewbon, and they act like it's a homecoming."

"What? Are you sure you saw the President's Chief of Staff get off an Iranian chopper in the mountains of Iraq?"

Some heavy chop caused them both to pause. Hudde, especially, seemed uneasy.

"Even in the dark, I know you're looking at me like I'm crazy, but I'm telling you I know what I saw."

"Pictures?"

"No, but if that wasn't bad enough, that's when we get jumped by a platoon-sized element. They didn't stumble upon us. They came up from over the mountain — right on top of us, Hudde. I'm telling you — they knew where we were. There is no evidence, but I'm telling you somebody gave us up."

They were now in deeper water, and unlike Gordan's mood, it was flat and calm. Nothing but the sound of wind and water interrupted their thoughts for the next twenty minutes.

Hudde reached out and grabbed Foster's arm. "Cut the engine!"

They floated in silence. Then the clouds parted, and the partial moon gave off enough light that they could make out a ship in the distance.

"That shape look like one of ours?" Hudde asked.

A ship ahead of them loomed large and ominous, a black cutout of a ship over blacker water in front of a blue-black background.

Foster allowed the smaller craft to drift toward the ship. "American cruiser," he finally pointed out.

Gordan stepped in to whisper to the taller man. "You're right. You'd better not tell anyone about this. You may be in danger. I'll do what I can to check into this."

Foster grabbed Hudde's forearm. "I've got five dead teammates who are depending on it. I thank you for them in advance — and thanks for saving my ass, too." Foster stared down into Hudde's face.

Hudde merely nodded and patted the taller man on the back as he climbed aboard the rescue ship.

Foster was escorted to sickbay to have his injuries checked, and Hudde went to the galley to get some coffee and run his hand over his beard. That's where the captain found him to let him know they would rendezvous with the rest of the fleet. Then, they'd catch a flight to Italy and, finally, make their way home.

2

Victor Crewbon strode confidently into the White House's Oval Office. The President, Lemme Dubois, stood staring out the window; he did not turn to make eye contact.

Being ultra-sensitive about his lack of height, Crewbon would not take a seat. He stood at the desk and waited for Dubois to face him. He was agitated and breathing hard; everyone on the White House staff tried to avoid Crewbon because of his renowned temper and cutting tongue. He knew that his behavior added fire to the "short-man-disease" whispers that floated around this administration, but he knew that, ultimately, this would be a reason for others to underestimate him.

His impatience caused him to rap on the desk with his knuckles to get the President to turn around.

"Come now, Victor. What has you so worked up?" the President asked.

Crewbon bowed his head and reached up to run a forefinger over a nasty scar that bisected his left eyebrow — an outward reminder of a sword fight from his youth. This was his "tell," as he did it instinctively anytime he was stressed.

"My problem?" He shook his head sadly. "Didn't you run an election campaign in which you promised to get America out of the Middle East?" He spoke to Dubois like he was a school child. "Didn't you promise peace? Haven't you instructed me to reach out and find you support from that region of the world?"

Dubois started to react, but Crewbon held up one finger, causing the president to pause.

"Did I stand before America and make such a promise? No, Mr. President — that was you. If you can't control the Department of Defense and put a halt to the drone-strike program, then I guarantee you that you will lose support from the states and groups that have pledged to me that they would support your plans, and..." he took a deep breath "... you will fail!"

Crewbon took a deep breath and spoke softer, dropping the "Mr. President." "Lemme, I had met with and made deals with the victim of last night's missile strike. When word of this gets out, how am I going to help you continue to get support?"

At just over six feet and rail thin, Dubois thought he cut a dashing figure of a fifty-seven-year-old man. His greying temples made him think of Clark Gable every time he looked into the mirror. He was old money, making the "Wealthiest People in the World" list every year, a fact made more humorous when he ran a campaign touting change for the "little guy." The staff had made all kinds of jokes about "*leaving* only change" for the little guy, but damn if it hadn't worked.

He wasn't worried about Crewbon's attitude. He had been with him since college and he knew his heart was in the right place.

He walked over and sat on the corner of the desk, still taller than the standing Crewbon.

"Victor, I'm sorry if this makes your life more difficult, but I can't allow the beheading of Christians to keep happening without any response. We still have to think about the next election as well as the mid-terms."

Crewbon was trying to rub the scar off his forehead. "Lemme, those people are interlopers, disaffected agitators — nothing more. Please don't allow them to turn this into a religious war."

"They were children, Victor. Do you understand the optics? We killed men who were cutting the heads off children. How is this going to be used against us?"

Victor wagged his finger at the president. "It can make you a hero here, but it will never make you the bringer of peace for the rest of the world. They probably will recruit a dozen more just like him after this."

Dubois gave in and took a seat at his desk. "Tell me this: when are these differing factions going to put together an organization that we can negotiate in the open with? When will they deliver enough peace for us to point to? I seem to remember that was *your* promise to *me* during the campaign."

Crewbon stood before the desk and folded his arms across his chest. "Several things have to happen. Russia is still willing to ship the arms into Iraq, and that will get you the support of the number two there — Abdulla. However, Russia wants you not only to just ignore any actions they take along their borders but to make public statements that recognize their rightful ownership of those territories. And though they have been oddly silent lately, oil will be a topic soon enough."

Dubois began to shake his head.

Crewbon put both hands down on the desk and sighed, continuing before the President could voice any concerns. "If you want to gain some significant ground, you would denounce the newest Israeli settlements or, maybe even better yet, remove a missile system as a sign to the world of your displeasure."

Dubois let out a deep breath. "I don't know. Let's think about how we can couch the Russian support and maybe get one of the cable networks to run a special on how that land has always belonged to Russia." He put one finger into the air as a new idea hit. "Maybe have some poor villagers there say they support Russian re-expansion — everything was better before, yada yada."

Crewbon nodded his approval. "Nice. Consider it done."

"On the other front, Israel just makes it too easy. I'll start crafting a statement now that talks about how their aggressive expansionism threatens the peace of the entire region. I'm going to have to put those cards on the table soon enough. If the prime minister has a problem, I'll broach the removal of the anti-missile system."

"They'll squawk."

"But have no recourse. Really, I'm growing weary of all this. Maybe we should offer the Tribe half of Michigan and take them out of the Middle East equation altogether." Dubois allowed a half smile to creep across his face.

"Never joke like that. We need Israel to play the foil, otherwise the Arabs, Muslims, and Persians will start killing each other in greater numbers." Seeing Dubois look a bit flustered, he added, "Besides, with the refugee numbers that Detroit has taken in, the Jews wouldn't know the difference."

Dubois held up his hand, palm out. "Alright, alright. We stay the course. Now about this cable interview." He slid a paper from the pile before him and tapped it several times. "If that idiot asks me anything they didn't include on this list…"

"Don't worry, Lemme. They love you on that network. You think you can work in that other stuff when you do that interview?"

Dubois nodded. "Why don't you reach out and let them know I'd love to make some real news on their cable network if only they would look into that Russian story for us."

"Got it." Crewbon turned to walk out of the Oval Office.

"Victor, when you have some time, go visit the senator and be sure to tell B.B. how important his son is to us. We need to make sure the hooks are in deep on him. His future support will be of the utmost importance."

"Yes, Mr. President." Crewbon shut the door behind him and walked past the receptionist without acknowledging her, as usual. Crewbon didn't like the Democrat's Senate leader, B.B. Kinkade. In fact, he considered him the most obnoxious ass he had ever met, and that was saying a lot, as Crewbon had spent his entire life in politics. His son, Terry, however, was a sneaky, petty, and rich pretty-boy with daddy issues — someone Crewbon could trust to distrust. Someone he could work with.

Dubois flinched a bit from the sound of the door slamming as Crewbon exited. He couldn't help but be impressed with him. After all the years they had known each other, meeting as fresh-men at Princeton, Crewbon never had let him down. Crewbon came from some mysterious wealth, but it was nothing compared to the Dubois old family wealth. Dubois' great grand-daddy had been one of the largest landowners in France, operating some in-credibly successful wineries. During WWII, the family had taken notice of America's financial strength and moved there, and they had quickly become marketing, capital, and banking giants. Even with all that common knowledge, Crewbon had still gotten one-term Senator Dubois elected president using wealth and class-war-fare tactics. Dubois smiled at the irony.

They had spent so many nights discussing why socialism had failed where it had been tried and why they could successfully pull it off. The idea was bringing peace to the Middle East and creating a true global oneness. Crewbon always told Dubois that he could read a teleprompter speech for the first time and make people believe that those words had been fretted over for years. Everyone would walk away believing that he was "with them," no matter what position they were for.

For the last eighteen months, Crewbon had been conducting clandestine and off-the-record back-channel meetings with every branch of Islam, from Sunni to Shia, and he had been having success. Dubois believed in the ability of every man to reason, and Crewbon believed in real peace in the Middle East. Dubois really believed that he would be credited with obtaining the peace and that, in the future, his name would be whispered alongside names like Kennedy. Hell, even Democrats would forget Kennedy if they could pull this off.

The Israelis were his biggest problem. Sure, there would be inter-faith bickering between Muslim countries, but no would care if Israel weren't sandwiched in between them. The world had given the Jews their homeland. Why couldn't they take it away? He was actually serious when he suggested to Crewbon that they give those fuckers Illinois or Detroit. Dubois laughed at his own thoughts.

Sure, the biggest losers in all this were probably the Jews and the Constitution. But you know what? *Fuck them both.* His name would live forever. He closed his eyes and imagined the headlines *President Lemme Dubois brings about world peace!*

How would anyone then be able to stop the rest of his agenda?

■ ■ ■

At the same moment, Gordan Hudde was sitting down with the deputy director of the CIA, John Stevens. Hudde was always amazed at the physical presence and prowess of the big man, even at age 60-something. Hudde would bet the deputy director could still kick some asses if he were so inclined, and he was pleased that the man always seemed happy with his after-action reports.

Stevens always demanded the "November Sierra" report from Hudde, which is grunt-speak for "No Shit," and Hudde appreciated that very much. The big black man was a former football lineman and Marine, but, for a jarhead, he was pretty quick-witted. Hudde smiled at the joke but didn't feel comfortable enough to make that comment out loud.

Because he was a former Marine, you would have thought he would be a vein-popping screamer, but that was the furthest thing from the truth. He seldom spoke above a gravelly whisper.

"Hudde, I've read your report." He folded his big hands on the desk. "Your mission failed."

Gordan sat up straighter and cleared his throat to defend his actions.

Stevens held up one big hand. "I hope I would have done the same thing, but that hasn't stopped the Director from climbing up my ass, and I don't appreciate it."

Gordan began to point, and again Stevens held up his hand in the universal "Stop" sign.

"Your report includes absolutely zero conversation that you and the rescued SEAL had on your trip back; I find that either inaccurate or unsettling. As an operator, wouldn't you look to gather information from that man for our benefit? You — one of the best I have in my employ — came up with nothing?"

Hudde began to take a deep breath and lean forward but was interrupted again; he shrugged his shoulders and leaned back into the hard-backed seat.

"So I requested the DoD report of the debrief of Jim Foster, and do you know what? No conversation in hours and hours of being together. You and a Navy SEAL you have worked with before, and no intelligence gleaned that maybe we would find useful?"

Gordan looked at his boss, waiting to see if now was the moment he was required to speak.

"Foster and his team were supposed to take out Farouq Mustafa, but while waiting to see who was coming in on an Iraqi helicopter, they were overrun."

"I knew that much; there is more." Stevens was staring.

"Sir, I need to be able to run with the information I'm about to share. I know you would want me to."

"We'll see."

Gordan leaned as far as he could over the desk, and Stevens leaned down as well, cocking his head to the side to listen with his "good" ear.

"Victor Crewbon and Terry Kinkade were there. Crewbon flew in on an Iranian chopper." Hudde sat back to watch his boss's reaction.

Stevens's eyes narrowed, and he leaned back into the plush leather chair, staring straight through Hudde.

He began nodding. "Even with who his daddy is, I gave Kinkade's worthless, self-entitled ass a boot on the way out of the door. Our director allowed him to stay on special assignment for Crewbon. I can tell you that Crewbon is one tough little bastard that I wouldn't trust as far as I could throw him." He leaned forward and dragged a big hand over what hair he had left on the top of his head.

"Iran? Russian involvement? Some kind of backdoor deal?" He looked up at the ceiling and bit his lower lip.

Hudde leaned in. "The SEAL, Foster, isn't saying anything about this, but obviously he believed that someone gave the enemy their position so that they couldn't report back what they saw. Without my dumb luck, no one would ever have known. I was hoping you'd cut me loose and let me run down whatever info I can."

Stevens began to think out loud. "You are correct — we must know what is going on." He pushed a forefinger right between his eyes as if he were pushing a button to begin thinking more clearly. "It would have to be totally off the books. If Director Smith catches wind of any operation, we're both screwed." Stevens's eyes focused on Hudde; he looked worried. "How about I get you some temporary work in South America? Maybe give you some time to nose around. But this is a two-man operation from here on out — right?"

"Yes, sir. Don't worry. I'll be careful." Hudde began to get up out of the chair. "Sir? You think Dubois knows? I mean that Crewbon is basically...well, you know — he's so far up his ass?"

Stevens stood and stretched out to his full height. "Listen, Gordan. You be careful. After a nuclear strike, there will be cockroaches and people like Crewbon — he's that kind of dangerous. You had better disappear after this meeting."

"Yes, sir."

3

Hudde accepted an official ride from the uniformed division in an underpowered, nondescript, dark official vehicle. No words were shared between the driver and Hudde. When he was dropped off at his Gainesville townhome, he merely rapped on the top of the car when he was safely out of the back seat.

Hudde walked to the front steps and dropped his duffle bag near the door. Then he inspected the frame, under the mat, and between the storm door without opening anything.

He walked around and inspected the grounds for obvious footprints. He peeked into the back patio door and looked for any signs that anyone had paid his home a visit during his latest absence. He was tired and this probably bordered on paranoia, but he had heard the horror stories of the lengths some had gone to take revenge on the agency in the past.

Returning to the front door, Hudde turned the key and slowly entered his sparsely furnished dwelling. Locking the door behind him, he entered the living room and went straight to the one piece of furniture that would go with him whenever he moved from here: his gun safe.

He pressed the buttons and opened the large, heavy door; the smell of the green felt and gun oil was comforting.

His oversized hand reached in and returned with his .45 ACP Springfield semi-auto handgun. The weight felt good and he immediately dropped the magazine from it, inspected that it was full, and set that magazine next to the other one that was fully loaded, standing upright inside the safe. Hudde pulled back on the slide and inspected the empty chamber; he slid a loose round into the chamber and allowed the slide to rack back. Then he slid home the loaded magazine and flicked the weapon off "Safe."

It took only seconds, as he had repeated this thousands of times. He could take that weapon, and many others, apart and then reassemble them — in the dark, if needed. Then he cleared his home, making sure that he was the only one present.

Hudde had no perishable items in his home; he took a meal-re-placement bar from the cupboard and washed it down with some tap water.

Returning to the safe, Hudde depressed a nearly invisible but-ton with the tip of a letter opener to slide a secret compartment in the safe wall open. He pulled a string and began pulling out thousands in cash as well as several different sets of identification, some created by the CIA and others he hoped were unknown by anyone in the government.

He slid his shoulder rig on and secured the .45 under his right arm. He leaned over and slid the ankle holster onto his ankle and strapped a small, five-round .38 caliber revolver into the padded holster. He really didn't like that gun because it was way too small for his hand, but he carried it just the same. He topped it all off with a couple of his favorite knives and headed into his bedroom to see about some clothes.

Carrying a medium-sized duffle out to his garage, Hudde closed the door, creating darkness in the windowless area. Flicking on powerful black lights, Hudde walked carefully around his pickup to ensure that there had been no intruders who'd walked through the powder that now glowed blue-white in the strange environment. Satisfied yet still cautious, Hudde checked the undercarriage and only then carefully opened the door, popped the hood, and checked inside the engine compartment. When he was satisfied, he threw the bag in the back cabin and climbed into the driver's seat. He repeated this ritual every time he returned from any overseas assignment. It was his intention never to be a star on the wall in the CIA lobby.

He liked the feel of sitting up a bit higher than many of the vehicles on the road, although there were more and more people driving around in big SUVs. Many of the men he had worked with were into fast cars, but he could count on one hand the times he had to drive much faster than 100 mph. Many times, he'd had to take some *improvised* routes while he worked. Plus he had always figured that, when he got old and retired, he would get himself a dog that never left his side — that would require a good truck.

Hudde reached up and opened the garage door. He turned to the south, figuring to get a room somewhere nearby, maybe near Fredericksburg Virginia. Maybe by then, he would get some word from Stevens. If there was nothing nefarious going on, then Stevens would find that out very quickly. Even if it was some back-channel secret plan, Hudde was confident that it would be ferreted out by Stevens and the resources that he had available.

If Stevens came up empty, if there was no whisper stream that Stevens could tap into to give a rational explanation for what

Foster had described, well, then, that is when it would really begin to worry Hudde. He wondered if Stevens would use his entire arsenal of legal and illegal information-collecting capabilities or would wait to see if Hudde could find something more concrete before he leaned out over his skis.

At the hotel, Hudde used the extra cash to get a room off the books. A huge movie fan, he gave his name as Harold Callahan, the same name as one of his new-nongovernment-approved ID cards.

Hudde sat in the small, uncomfortable chair near the third-floor window, staring out at the sky, looking at nothing. Most people did not understand what a thorough investigation looked like. A thorough investigation involved taking the whole of what is possible and slowly removing anything untrue or likely impossible. It is a painstakingly slow process made more difficult by lack of information or dependable witnesses.

A real diagram of a murder investigation, for example, would be a dot under a pyramid. The dot represents the actual crime and the base of the pyramid represents all the possibilities. Each time some suspect or aspect of the investigation was eliminated, you would have the next layer, with fewer options. In the end, you reach the pinnacle and one suspect.

Hudde did not question anything the Navy SEAL Jim Foster told him. He believed that two American government officials were meeting with the enemy. It was entirely speculation to link that meeting with the SEAL team being overrun and the subsequent capture of Foster. It also was entirely speculation that the meeting itself was illegal or criminal and not some back-channel attempt to catch an even bigger fish or create some kind of alliance that would manifest later in the administration's State Department, NATO, or a UN vote.

If that was the case, he knew that the men and women of the CIA would be able to give Stevens something that would point in the direction of a new secret plan. If not, the first thing Hudde would want to know is if he could somehow prove that Crewbon and Kinkade were actually in-country — even just figure out if they had a window of time to be there and back to begin with.

Hudde found a library and began to conduct some research on the movements of President Dubois over the time frame that would have been necessary. Hudde guessed a three-day window, at a minimum.

Dubois had spent some down time at Camp David. The article talked about the voracious reading appetite of this intellectual giant of a president. Hudde smiled knowing that currently Dubois was the media darling; he wondered what kind of headlines he would read if they turned on him.

There were a few video clips of Dubois walking through the White House grounds to get onto Marine One, giving a limp-wristed salute as he climbed the few steps into his ride. On one of those clips, Crewbon could be seen in the background. It appeared that no news was made by anyone for that entire week, and Hudde knew he would not be able to confirm if Crewbon was with the president the entire time.

Nothing in the media suggested that the President and his Chief of Staff were taking time off separately. For all anyone would know, they were together for a relaxing week.

His phone vibrated; he placed the earpiece into his ear and exited the library to speak outside, turning his back to the wind.

"Yes, sir," Gordan said. It was Stevens.

"Hudde, our people have nothing. I have tried to get information from some other sources, but I'm just not willing to go any further right now without some hard evidence."

"I understand." Hudde paused. "Any chance you'd let The Kid take a shot?"

Ivan "the kid" Mykhaylychenko was a late-20-something computer genius of Russian descent who had cracked every code, hacked every computer system, and, at one time, stolen quite a bit of money and was ultimately "convinced" to come work for the agency.

"No, not at this time." Stevens did not waver. "Have you gotten anything new?"

"No, but I've just started."

"I wouldn't give you a chance to start anything if it weren't for all the rumors surrounding this administration's relationships with some suspect groups; frankly, it does worry me at night. Just take it easy, and keep me informed — understood?"

"Lima Charley," Hudde said. They both understood that military code for "Loud and Clear."

Hudde took a cab to a car rental and rented a dark Ford Taurus. Then he went back to the hotel to clean up a little and put on the one suit and tie that he owned. He hated getting dressed up, especially if he had to wear the tie; he hated the feeling around his neck. He'd also never spent the money to have the suit fitted. When a guy his size got a shirt that fit his twenty-inch neck and large shoulders, two men could fit into the waist. He had to cram all that extra cloth down into his pants, making them uncomfortable as well.

Within minutes, he looked like he'd slept in the suit, but he felt it wouldn't hurt because that would make him look like an underpaid FBI field agent, as his ID stated. He would make his way onto Bolling, Andrews, and then Dover Air Bases to see if he could find a flight out during the dates in question.

Hudde was positive that he had narrowed the possible flight out to a three-day window in October.

The Non-Commissioned Officer in Charge (NCOIC) at Bolling did not hesitate when the rumpled-looking Agent Callahan flashed his badge and complained about all the hours wasted having to run down some information about some flights out. Hudde bitched about getting the bullshit jobs and shared a cup of coffee with the NCOIC as they went over the logs, looking for fictitious dignitaries while Hudde scanned for the names of Crewbon or Kinkade to be on the manifest.

The NCOIC nodded as if this was a fairly regular occurrence, and she seemed genuinely happy to have someone to talk to for a half-hour. Hudde thanked her and head out toward Andrews.

Andrews Air Base turned out to be a lot busier and a much different experience. The NCOIC came out to meet Hudde and shake hands, but his attitude was much more suspicious. He stated that there was absolutely a zero chance that he would allow agent Callahan to review any official document without written authorization from his commanding officer.

"Absolutely no way that I would need a hard copy of anything, sergeant. If you do have the information I'm looking for, then I'll be happy to get my boss to contact yours and make it all above board and everything. I just need a look to see if we really need to jump through all those hoops." Hudde wrinkled his nose and shrugged his shoulders.

The NCOIC shook his head. "Nope — we jump through all those hoops first here, Agent Callahan. Why don't you let me copy your ID and make sure we can reach out to you after we get all the required documentation?"

"Sure." Hudde smiled a bit sheepishly and handed over the identification card, upset that he would have to cut that one up later. "Here is my card; I'll call you when my superior has had the time to make all the arrangements."

Hudde made an exit and drove north and west until he stopped in Harrisburg, Pennsylvania, getting a room there. He had been weighing if he should call the commanding officer at Andrews tomorrow and claim that they had found the flight information at another base. Then he shot down that thought process as well. Hudde also realized that Crewbon was not known to travel without the President, so it was unlikely that they would disguise a trip like this as official business, and, therefore, there was a very good chance that they would not take a military flight. There would be too many chances that a FISA request would uncover something they did not want in the open. No, Crewbon would take a private flight from a private airstrip.

Tomorrow he would start looking at small, private airports. He cussed himself for making a mistake and wasting precious time.

4

Victor Crewbon leaned back, sitting on his heels, kneeling on the floor of his minimal apartment. He closed his eyes and held his hands palms up, praying for ultimate victory.

He opened his eyes and rolled up his prayer rug, storing it in a cabinet. Strict adherence to his faith could be overlooked as he practiced *Al Takeyya* — "the deception of the unwashed and unbelieving in an effort to advance Islam."

At one time, his plan had been to send himself to Allah and reap his reward by taking out many of the most important people in the heart of the great Satan, but as he had advanced, the plan had changed. He would not be able to tell you when he had begun to believe that Allah had a greater mission for him than that of Martyr. But now he believed he would end up Caliph and world leader of those who follow the prophet — peace be upon him. He had successfully pushed Dubois to reach for greater things; why not do the same for himself?

He had no TV or radio, there was no noise to clutter his mind, and now he understood what needed to be done next.

He reached into a cupboard and pulled out a blanket that was rolled tight. He unrolled it onto the floor, and pockets that were sewn into it became visible — ten in all.

Crewbon selected the third one and pulled out the phone and the battery, which was stored separately. He reassembled them and rang the one number that had been programmed.

"Yes," came across the speaker.

"Your plan has changed. You and your team will search out and question a man who was in the wrong mountain range in a remote area. My brother, this man is not important, but his information is. Understood?"

"Yes."

"I must know what he has told his superiors about his last mission. Make no mistake, he is a dangerous man who works for the great Satan; you will take care so that you can carry out the rest of our plans."

"Of course. His will be done."

"*Allahu Akbar,*" Crewbon said before reciting an address in Texas. He ended the call and then broke the phone down into three parts, to be destroyed later.

Crewbon put on a pot for tea and then allowed his mind to drift back over the thirty-six years that he had been actively working on his plan. He had pushed, prodded, cheated, and allowed himself to at times be humiliated to get to the point he was at today, the right-hand man to the President of the United States.

He would never forget meeting Dubois those many years ago at the university. Dubois, of course, was a simpleton, a very wealthy idiot, who, coming from a position of ridiculous money, seemed interested only in gaining power. Crewbon had recognized it instantly and had made himself Dubois' best friend and confidant for their entire time at school. Crewbon had become the most important person to Dubois—the voice of reason, the bringer of wisdom, the key to Dubois' success. Whenever Dubois drifted into his dreams of an American Socialist Utopia, Crewbon had reined him in and pushed him to stay within acceptable discourse. Crewbon was the man holding the strings to a puppet.

When Dubois had that problem their senior year with that drunken freshman, it was Crewbon who'd got his hands dirty. It wouldn't be the last time Crewbon would get blood on his hands, but it was the first time that Dubois acknowledged that he owed everything to Crewbon.

Thirty-six years later, Crewbon still believed Dubois was a moron, but it was his family name that had allowed Victor Crewbon to travel the world and build alliances. From the slums of London to royalty in Saudi Arabia, believers both Sunni and Shia had begun to believe in Crewbon as well. Crewbon believed that the final phase of his plan would bring in even the Wahhabi and that one third of the globe would live within the new Caliphate; the entire old-world hierarchy would begin to crumble.

They had developed footholds in nearly every nation; only China remained mostly unchanged, but one day they would be alone against the rest of the Muslim world.

The teapot whistled him back to the present, and, as he poured the steaming water, he wondered about the security briefing at the end of the day in which the FBI had been concerned about someone "probing" military airbases. He knew it was not one of his people; he was concerned, for he hoped no plans from a lone wolf would interrupt his own. He shrugged his shoulders and sat looking out into the night. Even he made assumptions based on the reports that the man had been bearded; he smiled at the thought that he had become Islamophobic.

Crewbon knew that the FBI would be angry that someone was impersonating an agent; they would take it personally and get the guy. That would be okay. His plans would not be interrupted.

■ ■ ■

Lemme Dubois slipped into bed at the White House; he really slept much better after his wife had moved into another bedroom. He could read or watch TV without her incessant need to be involved in all his decisions. Not satisfied to take up some small program or needy charity, his wife wanted to be part of his administration. While she said all the right things about helping the poor and downtrodden, she just didn't see the optics of throwing all the lavish black-tie balls and parties. He had even begun to prohibit journalists from being able to cover her events so that they would either get favorable stories or, better yet, none at all.

He had believed, as she fervently still did, during college, but now after years in government service, touring the world, he no longer believed...as much. He didn't mind setting up a program or two if he knew money would somehow help his next election, though.

They had also begun to argue about his relationship with Victor. While she should not challenge Crewbon based solely on what she had observed firsthand during Lemme's elections, she surely would not if she truly understood *everything* he had done for him, going all the way back to their college days.

In a fit of anger, she had even suggested that they were homosexual when Lemme would not share information regarding some issue — he couldn't even remember what it was all about.

He shook his head. Now, with the all the wrangling, all the threats and promises behind them, Dubois was positive that he was going to get a new peace deal signed in the Middle East, and that was following the announcement of a deal with Iran regarding nuclear power and weapons.

He could admit here, to himself, that the Iranian deal would never have been accomplished without Crewbon. Crewbon was brilliant at handling all the players as well as being able to interpret conversation; he had made the Secretary of State look somewhat useless in the process. The way the people reacted as they left the negotiations in Russia, Dubois felt he may be able to run against the supreme ruler himself — and win! He now was working feverishly to get the treaty ratified by Congress.

Surely, nearly everything ever done in secret comes to light, especially if a Republican were to win the next presidential election. But his approval ratings were hovering around sixty percent, and, if a deal in Israel were to be signed, the Republican didn't stand a chance. His back-channel deals with Russia regarding Syria and Iran were safe for another four to six years, and, then if or when they were uncovered, it would be far too late. The history books would already be written — his own biographer, with the help of the Department of Education, would see to that.

Dubois slipped back onto the pillows, folding his arms behind his head. Maybe during the next four years, he would be able to finally create a single-payer healthcare system; so many had tried and failed in the past. He would not be able to accomplish everything he and his wife dreamt about so many years ago, but it would be a great start. He closed his eyes and dreamt about the people rising up to make him dictator for life; a smile spread across his face. Surely then he would get some things done. He slept well.

■ ■ ■

Gordan Hudde set down the FBI background report on Victor Crewbon that director Stevens had been able to get to him. Hudde now understood why Stevens had found the report lacking; it had very little of interest in it, especially for a man who was so close to the president of the United States.

The report followed briefly Crewbon's work history back to his college days, where he had met and befriended Lemme Dubois. The family background told of a very large and successful importing and exporting business in Greece with depots in Russia all the way down through the Middle East; the grandfather, Aeneas Crewbon, had started and grown this all on his own. The father, Andrei, it seemed, had no interest in the family business. While it appeared that he was a bit revolutionist and anti-capitalistic in what would have been Victor's youth, he had been more than happy to sell the business upon his father's death and reap the rewards of his father's hard work.

Victor Crewbon's mother, Mary — last name "Johnson" — had no other information available; *odd*.

Hudde sat on his hotel bed, grabbed his chin, and pulled down and through his beard; he looked down at his own phone.

He knew that he was not supposed to call the Kid directly, but this may be something important. He convinced himself and dialed.

"I'm supposed to report all agent contacts to the director himself," Ivan "the Kid" Mykhaylychenko said immediately upon answering.

Hudde's brows furrowed. "You know who this is?"

"Da."

"I'll never make another call, I promise. But I need a little help, maybe with an answer that could be gotten from the IRS?"

"This interests me. I will not hang up."

"If you could dig up anything interesting about a 'Mary Johnson' and her eventual husband, Andrei Crewbon — maybe when they first filed, home purchases, and maybe where I could find Mary now. Her husband is dead."

Hudde heard plastic keys being tapped for an answer. "You can call me back anytime you come up with something."

No response. Hudde wondered if he should just hang up.

"1980," the Kid finally said.

"Okay, 1980 what?"

"That is when the married Mary and Andrei Crewbon first filed taxes from a new home, purchased in Michigan."

"You..."

The Kid interrupted. "It is also the year that Andrei received his American citizenship. Also, you should be made aware that Mary is gone now as well. The only surviving family is Mary's mother, Melissa Johnson, currently residing in a nursing home near the former family home in Columbus, Ohio."

"Are you kidding me? You got all that just now?" The plastic keys never stopped tapping in the background.

"May I return to *my* work now, Mr. Hudde?"

"Well you're so good at this — no. I have another issue."

"What else can I do for you?"

"Without driving around to every airport in the region, how could I find a private plane heading to a specific area?" Hudde crossed his fingers, hoping that the Kid would be interested.

"Oh, that's too easy; they would file a flight plan with the FAA."

Gordan cleared his throat. "Sure, but you know, without asking the FAA, would you be able to find a flight out of the country, say, landing in Afghanistan or Syria?"

"Mr. Agent, a flight landing in either of those countries would be kept secret due to 'verifiable threats' — the language adopted in a law passed in the year 2000." It sounded like the Kid was really abusing the keys to his keyboard. "And ultimately that is why I have found the flight you are looking for — at the Charlottesville Albemarle Airport — so easily."

"Amazing. Thanks, Kid."

That fucker scares me, Hudde thought. It was highly probable that the Kid was somehow still listening.

Without needing to search to verify if a flight had actually gone out, Hudde had personal contacts in Greece he felt he should go see. The nearly empty Victor Crewbon background concerned him, but he was much closer to Ohio and the connection to farm country in flyover country, and that interested Hudde nearly as much. How the hell did those two people meet and marry?

5

A rooster tail of dust followed a small pickup truck near the town of La Mesa in south Texas. The driver pulled into a retail construction site and bumped along the dirty and broken pavement toward a white van. The sun hadn't been up for long, and the air was a brisk forty-eight degrees, but that didn't keep the three dark, tough-looking men from standing outside and waiting for their two compatriots.

A phone chain had started late yesterday, telling each man where to wait and what the vehicle looked like that would be picking them up. No one at the Home Hardware store would have noticed that some of the men did not approach each vehicle but had waited for one in particular before they became interested and were ultimately allowed in.

The men at the van went by the names of "Chuck," "Eddy," and "Dan"; however, those were not their real names. They had snuck across the porous US border with the Mexican and other Central or South American illegals. Bob, who was just climbing from behind the truck's driver's seat, had been here the longest.

He had waited patiently for the call that had come just yesterday — *three long years* he had waited — and now his cell was finally being activated. Andy, the fifth and last of his men, stepped from the passenger side of the pickup and greeted his fellow jihadist.

"*Allahu akbar*," he said quietly.

They had known of each other but did not meet. They had not missed work when they had it, and they had done nothing to draw attention to themselves. They were of one mind, and that was to strike fear into the heart of the great Satan on behalf of Islam. They were the shock troops that would help bring America to its knees.

Bob nodded at the van, and the four other men got inside. Bob had left the van here as a rally point last night and had stolen the construction-company truck to pick up Andy. But the construction guys would find the truck, keys under the floor mat, with no damage and nothing missing except a little gas, so the sheriff wouldn't be called. They would figure that some local kids were out messing around.

About six miles east of the town, Bob recognized the mile marker he was looking for as well as the tree out in the pasture that stood alone. He pulled over on the south side of the road. Bob turned on the four-way emergency flashers and climbed into the back with the others.

He opened a large cardboard box and removed two magnetic signs, handing one each to Dan and Eddy. He then handed a folded military entrenching tool to Chuck and waved for him to follow. They hopped the two-strand barbed-wire fence and walked in the direction of the large gray oak, with its distinctive double trunk. Bob noticed a large billboard just down the road that advertised eight hundred acres of cattle ranch for sale; it was good they got what they came for now, otherwise they may have lost what they came for.

Bob found the large, flat rock under the tree that he was looking for. He pointed at the ground there, and Chuck broke ground just as a murder of crows flew overhead. Bob looked up at them and nodded.

Two feet down, Chuck hit something hard and uncovered the end of a steel footlocker. He worked to clear one end completely and then pulled hard to unearth the rest. Bob quickly grabbed the other end's handle, and they carried it back to the waiting white van, which now sported new signs for a florist that did not exist.

Bob and Chuck dragged the footlocker into the back of the van. They slammed the doors closed, and Bob was in the driver's seat and moving forward in seconds. They covered the footlocker with an old blanket, and then Andy and Chuck used it as a seat; no one spoke.

■ ■ ■

Hudde walked the quiet neighborhood where he guessed Mary Johnson had played and grown up. The houses were far enough apart and had large-enough lawns that one neighbor would have to really work to know the other's business. Good fences.

Hudde knocked on some doors, trying to find anyone that knew the Johnsons. On the third door, an elderly gentleman came outside after slipping on a worn-and-patched Carhartt jacket. A yellow lab pushed his nose into Hudde's groin until the man called him over to an old rocker on the corner of the front porch.

He told Hudde that he didn't ever see the daughter after she went off to school many years ago. The lab's tail thumped out a beat onto the porch's bare wood floorboards as the old man's weathered and age-spotted hand patted his head.

He told Hudde that Melissa Johnson was near his age but didn't seem to do well after the husband had passed. He thought she was in a facility on the other side of town named after some Catholic order.

Gordan thanked the man and patted the friendly dog goodbye.

Hudde crossed the town in his small rental, coming upon the brick single-story nursing home. It appeared to be a large square building; he parked in the front and walked into the main lobby.

The receptionist was on the phone. Hudde stood nearby, close enough to be annoying if it was a personal call. He guessed it was when the woman whispered into the phone and hung up.

"Can I help you?" she asked Gordan with a tone that told him that she was not all that interested in whether she could or not.

He glanced at her name badge. "Sue, a long time ago, I made a promise to a friend that I would talk to her mom for her, Melissa Johnson. I was traveling through town after all these years, and I would love to sit with her a spell if I could."

Sue's eyes gave away that she knew exactly who Gordan was asking for. "I'm afraid she's on our secure side. Are you family?"

"As you probably are aware, there is no family left; it's been weighing on me that I never followed up. I would appreciate a few minutes."

Sue looked a bit exasperated but clicked a button on a stainless-steel console with a microphone that snaked up and curved towards her. "Cassandra, we have a visitor up front when you have a moment. Cassandra, up front, please."

She smiled a fake smile, and Gordan thanked her and stepped over to a glass case holding photos of the residence at birthdays,

Christmas, and other festive occasions, all with colorful balloons and other decorations fitting for the occasions. Hudde found it disconcerting that he had survived so much in his life just to realize that surviving meant he could be in a place like this one day.

A large black female in bright-pink scrubs came out from the far side interior doors and walked up to Sue at the desk. There were a few minutes of whispering, and then the woman turned and walked up to Gordan, holding her chin up high.

"How can I help you, sir?" Her name badge showed that she was indeed Cassandra. She was nearly as tall as Gordan, and he imagined that she probably outweighed him, too; she seemed strangely light on her feet as she approached.

Hudde gave her his best "Aw, shucks" smile and gave her the same story that he had told Sue just moments ago.

"Mister?" It was a question.

"Oh, I'm sorry. My name is 'Harold,' but everyone calls me 'Harry.' I promise I won't take long."

Cassandra sighed like a tour guide starting another tour with the same spiel. "Melissa has Lewy bodies dementia; do you know anything about that disease?"

Gordan shook his head, and she continued.

"It's a form of Alzheimer's, but it is not the same. Melissa sometimes has a very good grasp on the past, but her short-term memory is gone. The dementia often controls what she sees and hears, and sometimes she will get into full-blown arguments with someone who is not there. Maybe she acknowledges you, maybe not; it all depends on the day. If you agitate her, even at no fault of your own, it may set her off all day. You still want to see her?"

Gordan grabbed his chin, wondering. "If it's okay, yes. I think I still should try."

"Follow me, then." They headed toward the steel double doors closest to the main desk. "This is the secure wing." She waved her magnetic card, and the door lock released with an audible *Clank!*

Hudde followed Cassandra into the hall on the opposite side of the secure doors. He was immediately struck by the urine and disinfectant smell which combined for something even worse — most likely death. Some of the elderly seemed to be bed-ridden. Hudde caught a quick image of them lying in their beds through slightly open doors. Others used walkers in the hall, heading to some unknown location. Hudde guessed there had to be a day room with a TV and game boards somewhere. He had seen *One Flew Over the Cuckoo's Nest*.

Hudde wanted to turn and leave, never to look back.

Cassandra stopped at a door and turned, waiting for Hudde. "If she gets agitated, please pull that string there to notify some-one, and then just leave. Okay?"

"Sure."

Cassandra stepped in and talked quietly. "Melissa, a friend of your daughter has come to see you today. Isn't that nice?"

Gordan took that as his cue and walked into the room. It was very sparse with a hospital bed, one small dresser, and a small TV that hung on a wall mount. A single door inside was open, and Hudde could see a white porcelain sink.

Melissa Johnson was seated in a chair that looked out a small window into what Gordan guessed was a common area in the cen-ter of the facility. It was open to the sky so that no one wandered off, he imagined.

Melissa Johnson didn't acknowledge Cassandra or Gordan. In fact, there was no movement, and Hudde wondered if he had missed her altogether. Her white hair was so thin that he could see the pink and aged-spotted scalp; an oxygen hose wrapped around and under her nose to a tank on a two-wheeled carrier at her side.

Cassandra called her name two times before reaching out to touch her shoulder. "Missy. Missy."

Melissa Johnson suddenly sat up straighter and yelled out in a strong voice that any drill sergeant would have been proud of. Gordan flinched.

"I said I'm not hungry!"

"I already took your tray away, Missy. You have a visitor." Cassandra shrugged her shoulders and pointed at the string before stepping out. Gordan nodded.

"Mrs. Johnson, I knew your daughter. I used to work with her." Gordan was making it up as he went along.

"Lazy child never worked a day in her life."

Gordan was amazed at her sudden lucidity. "Well, she wanted me to tell you that she loves you if I ever saw you."

Melissa Johnson snapped her head around, looking past Hudde. Her eyes narrowed, and her brows furrowed. She grimaced, showing a lot of gums and one or two teeth. She took a cane from nearby and used it to point past Hudde, out into the hall.

"Darla, if you come in here to take my stuff, I'm going to whack you good!" She waved the cane to emphasize her point.

Hudde was afraid to move, and it gave him chills down his back as he looked out into the empty space.

"You sure scared her away." Gordan wondered if that would work. It did.

"She always comes back, though." She looked about the room, her eyes seeming to focus. "Where is my damned lunch? You'd swear they were trying to starve me."

Gordan leaned forward. "Mrs. Johnson, I was wondering about the birth of your grandson."

"Never met him." She began to rock back and forth in her chair.

"Your daughter never brought your grandson or her husband back home to meet her parents?"

Melissa Johnson turned and made eye contact with Gordan. "She went off to school and married that foreign darkie; I never saw her again. Never saw any of them except some pictures. Now they're all dead, and I don't care."

Gordan wanted to correct her. Her grandson was very much alive. But her eyes focused behind him, and her breathing seemed to speed up. Her knuckles turned even whiter as she gripped the cane tightly.

She swung the cane in an arc that would have struck Gordan in the head if he hadn't moved.

"Darla — you bring my money back!" Her oxygen hose fell from her nose, and the cane struck the back of the chair that Gordan was sitting in.

He jumped up and backed toward the door.

The nurse stepped back into the room and tried to calm the diseased and frail woman. Gordan stepped back into the hall, hoping that he didn't run into "Darla" in the process.

Cassandra stepped up into Gordan's space and whispered that maybe he should go now. Gordan was more than happy to leave this place.

In his car, Gordan closed his eyes. *Was this your reward for making it to old age — sitting in your own waste and not knowing if your demons were real or imagined?*

Maybe being remembered by a star on the wall wasn't such a bad way to go.

He didn't think this trip was going to bear any fruit for his investigation. Having a child disappear from a small town and never coming back was no crime. It probably happened all the time. Being estranged from your parents probably happened more often than most people knew.

Determined to find any nugget of information about Victor Crewbon, Hudde headed out to find the old high school. Inside, he asked if they had old yearbooks on hand. They did, and he looked through the early 1960s, looking for Melissa Johnson, which was incorrect, as that was her married name.

Nineteen sixty-two was a class of a little more than eighty students. He found a fresh-faced, very-serious-looking "Melissa Venters" standing tall in the back of a class picture, arms folded across her chest.

He jotted down some names of girls in her class and one boy she was pictured with heading out to a dance. He moved outside to use his phone to search for a possible local address, wondering if anyone had stayed here through adulthood.

Thomas Chandler was listed, not far outside of town. It was Hudde's third stop, and, while the others had remembered fondly for a moment, no one had anything to offer. Hudde was leaving after this stop, regardless.

This stop turned out better than the others — not just for the information that was offered but for the vibrant seventy-six-year-old woman he met on the step of the old farmhouse.

Teresa Chandler was happy to have a visitor. She may have been a bit lonely, but she was a healthy, bright-eyed woman — and the exact same age as the frail and feeble Melissa Johnson he had seen earlier in the day.

She offered him a seat on the wind-chilled front porch and went inside to get some coffee. Gordan watched the empty rope swing dance in the wind while he waited.

She returned with strong, hot coffee in brown ceramic heavy mugs. It felt good in Gordan's hand.

"So you say you're doing some research on Melissa Johnson's grandson?"

"That's right, Mrs. Chandler. I'm afraid that Mrs. Johnson couldn't really help."

Geese in perfect formation flew over the house, and she looked up and took a sip of her coffee.

"Melissa Venters," she said softly as she remembered. "I remember us in high school." She looked to the sky again. "Poor thing. I heard a while ago that she wasn't well. She was my main rival, you know. She was chasing hard after my Tom our senior year of high school."

Gordan wanted to encourage her without slowing down her thought process. "Oh, really," he said as he took a sip from his own mug.

"Oh, my Tom was the star football player, big, strapping, and good-looking boy." She kept watching the geese while she spoke. "His daddy had this here farm, and I knew Tom would take it over one day. I had life all planned out."

She turned now to make eye contact with Gordan. "Anyway, you *think* you have it all figured out…" she faded away for a moment "You just don't know."

Gordan nodded.

"She was wispy thin and so light on her feet, like a dancer. I was a bit jealous, but I once had that thick black hair and boobs going for me." She smiled and sat up straight to emphasize the point. "Now my back just hurts." She barked laughter at her own joke.

Gordan smiled but looked down.

"Oh, don't lie to me young man. Sex and food — it's all you men care about. It don't matter if you're a farmer or the head of a bank."

Gordan turned his hands palms up in front of him and smiled a bit sheepishly. "Is there anything else?"

She barked out another short laugh and pushed his knee with her foot, nearly spilling his coffee.

"Not for the male of the species." She laughed out loud again. "Yeah, we were rivals back then, but I won, you can clearly see. She denied it to me once, but when her daughter ran away with that man during college, I think it done ruined her." She nodded, agreeing with her own point.

"Do you think she, I mean the daughter, ever came to visit and maybe brought her grandson?" Gordan asked.

"If it happened, I never heard about it. Once you denounce America, call Reagan a fascist, I guess you don't come visit round here." She raised an eyebrow, waiting for Gordan.

"The daughter went a bit radical?"

"She was always a bit political, I guess, but she was never the same after going to college. And then, of course, she met that foreign kid and ran off." She took another sip of her coffee and then looked down at her shoes before looking back up and shrugging her shoulders. "That's all Melissa ever said to me. I couldn't tell you anything else."

Gordan drained the good black coffee. "That's way more than I knew before, Mrs. Chandler. I appreciate it very much." He stood and shook her hand while she remained seated. "Thank you for the information and the good strong coffee." He nodded at her and walked to his rental. *"And for being such a healthy person,"* he said under his breath. It was so refreshing to talk to her after the experience of the nursing home.

Gordan turned and headed for the airport, thinking about the sixteen-year-old Victor Crewbon showing up on American soil for the first time. Coming from where? And, more importantly, what was his attitude toward his adopted country? Did he rebel against his parents or possibly develop even more of an anti-American attitude?

Gordan had a contact in Greece, and he needed to find out all he could about the relationship from the grandfather there to the father. He made the appropriate calls and planned for some travel.

6

Victor Crewbon stood looking out the window of the Democratic leader's office window.

"You know, when you came to me with your concerns about your son, BB, I had more than a few doubts myself." He turned to look at Senator Kinkade and paused for dramatic effect. "His ability to find and make the contacts he has over the last year has been key to everything the President is trying to accomplish with the Middle East. You should be very proud."

BB Kinkade stood and stepped over to the fine crystal carafe. "I'll drink to that." He poured only one glass, for he knew that Crewbon did not drink. "I told you, the kid's smart. He aced everything in college, and I assure you the grades were all on his own. I never had to bribe anyone for that." He raised his glass and downed the amber liquid.

Kinkade continued. "I was really worried there for a time. He was so angry, and I made sure he had everything." He looked at Victor and shrugged. "The parade of women?" Again he shrugged.

"Well it's good to hear, Victor. Thank you — and the President, of course."

Victor thought about what he was going to say next. "A man has to find his niche, I think, before he can reach his potential. I didn't see how the Army or the Agency was going to help him. Now, there is nothing but promising possibilities on his horizon."

Kinkade joined Crewbon at the window but closed his eyes, as he appeared to be looking outward. He shook his head slowly as he spoke. "I was shocked when he enlisted. I didn't know what he was thinking."

Victor reached up and patted Kinkade on the center of his back. "Well, it's all behind you now." He started walking to the dark mahogany door. Stopping before he reached for the handle, he turned back to Kinkade. "I understand that the President is a little more progressive than you are, Senator, but he still plans to aggressively change America for the good. Next Friday, when he addresses the United Nations, his proposals will fire up the right, but we know that, with you and your son's support, we will successfully enact his proposed legislation. We really need you out there supporting his Middle East peace plan."

Kinkade stepped closer to his desk. "Israel and many of their supporters are never going to come around to this plan, Victor. Many on our side believe it will be career suicide."

Crewbon took two steps closer, faster than the senator could have imagined. BB took a half step backwards.

Crewbon ran a finger over the scar in his eyebrow before speaking. "Tell me, Senator. How many *true* believers do you have in your caucus? One or two? Stop with the ridiculous posturing. Get your ass out there and pull your people along. Trust me — after the President's address at the UN, you will begin to see support change in the polls."

Kinkade didn't want to argue, but he did want to make a point. "We have elections to worry about, while you can coast for another year, year and a half."

Crewbon sighed. "Christ, Kinkade — how many decades have you been here? You're in your late seventies?" Crewbon shook his head. "Don't you have enough streets or libraries named after you back home?"

Kinkade walked past Crewbon to the door, waiting there to show this conversation was about over. "Listen, Victor. I'm pushing and pulling these people toward your finish line. The President can be assured that we are doing everything we can."

Crewbon checked his tie as he walked back to the door. "Peace in the Middle East by Christmas this year. How do you think *that* will affect your members' election chances?"

Kinkade nodded. "You guys pull that off, and we'll secure a Democratic congress for the next twenty years." He smiled just saying that.

Crewbon nodded. "*We*, Senator—me, you, your son Terry, and the president—*we* are going to get it done!"

Crewbon stopped and made a gesture for the senator to lean down.

"Listen, Senator. This is beyond top secret. It's part of a plan that's still in its early stages. I need your assurance that this stays here."

BB frowned. "Of course."

"When our plans are finalized, the President will sign an agreement with the supreme ruler in Iran. We will have the support of most of the Arab nations and many different factions of Islam. It will be historic, and you could be there. Think of your own legacy."

Kinkade stepped back. "But how can this be? I've heard nothing of this!"

Crewbon stepped further into Kinkade's personal space. "And remember — you *still* know nothing of this." He studied Kinkade's face, feeling that he had gotten the desired response. "I'll reach out to you when the time draws near, and you'll tell me which side of history you will want to stand on at that time." He patted Kinkade on the chest a couple of times before he exited the room.

■ ■ ■

Terry Kinkade was still working under the umbrella of the CIA, but he answered now only to Victor Crewbon or the President himself. While he was stateside, Terry felt a power that was literally indescribable.

His father, BB Kinkade, was probably one of the richest and most powerful men in America, and, as the "King of Congress," maybe the most recognizable, too. And Terry was quickly taking advantage of all the opportunities that had offered themselves up.

His time in the Middle East was, at times, frightening. But it took only one drone strike for Terry to convince many that they should be paying him for "protection" and, of course, what would happen if they did not. His own personal wealth skyrocketed during his tours there.

He was positive that Crewbon was aware of his extracurricular activities but was, so far, completely ignoring them. Besides, Crewbon was up to his own tricks that Terry went along with as well.

The Rolls-Royce Ghost that he was driving was one of the first major purchases that he had made with entirely his own money; it was his baby. Silver and gray, it turned heads wherever he drove it. He turned back into the Baltimore Four Seasons, where he had been living since he'd been in his early twenties — on his father's money. Heading down into the private parking garage, he opted for the valet to wash it first.

He stepped out and handed the car's fob to the young man at the booth there. At the same time, he slid a $100 bill into the man's uniform vest, patting it afterwards, just in case he hadn't noticed.

"I won't be heading out until late morning tomorrow. Make sure it's washed and ready for me." He began to step away but then turned back and patted the young man's face several times to get his attention. "And be very careful..." he pointed right at the kid's nose. "If you know what's good for you." He smiled and winked as he spun back, heading toward the lobby.

He was fairly tall and handsome, wearing a dark suit in the $2000 range, but no one would even remember him after getting sight of his escort tonight. Her service had told Terry "never again" after a few earlier incidents, but promising three times the normal pay seemed to loosen them up.

She was near six foot herself in four-inch heels, and her long, golden hair reflected lights as it cascaded over her bright-red dress. The slit up her leg meant that every man who caught sight of her walking in *kept* watching, waiting to see if she was going to expose a lacy undergarment; she knew that would be impossible. If you followed the seam all the way up the back of her leg to the silky lace of her hose at her thigh, there was nothing else to see.

This was something that Terry Kinkade enjoyed more than almost anything else. Years of being a dancing monkey for parties and events that his father held, he now strode through causing murmurs and angry glances from wives and drawing envy from the men. He wished he could listen to the arguments that would inevitably ensue. He'd watched it ruin dinners for some; he smiled at the purposeful havoc he helped cause.

The *maitre'd* held out the young woman's chair and couldn't help but look as she nearly exposed an entire leg as she sat; she pretended to blush and pulled her dress back over, tucking most of her leg out of sight.

"Cashmere, darling, the men are about to lose control. My lord, we may have a riot."

Terry turned and caught several of the men gawking; so did the wives or girlfriends.

Terry unbuttoned his jacket but did not take it off; he took his own seat. His handgun was comfortable under his left arm, and the jacket kept it concealed. Sometimes he would find faces he disliked and daydream about pulling the Walther semi-auto and shooting them — just to watch the rest of the "important" people flee in horror.

Terry came out of his trance to find Cashmere speaking to him. He did a bit of a double-take, and his eyes opened wide.

"Oh, I was so excited to be coming to the Four Seasons. One of my friends…"

Kinkade held up his hand to stop her.

"Cashmere, Darling. You have played your part here perfectly. You look beyond fantastic in that dress and…" he leaned in so that he could speak in a way that the other guests would not overhear "Every man in the place wants to fuck you."

She leaned back in her seat a bit, but Terry slid even closer.

"I'm not paying you by the word, right?"

She looked questionably at him. "But most men want…"

He shut her down again. He closed his eyes while he shook his head. "Cashmere, you're just not that bright, are you? So listen up. After we order, you are going to shut the fuck up. If you truly are unaware, I'll clear it up for you. I am not paying you by the word.

I'm paying you for your genetics — those fabulous legs and ass. So the next time your mouth opens, well, you know. Am I clear?"

She started to say something, but he cocked his head, and she just nodded.

"Oh, that's so much better." He smiled. "Hey maybe you can walk around the room to go powder your nose and give them all another show." He nodded and winked.

■ ■ ■

Sometime near two-thirty in the morning, a disheveled-looking Cashmere entered the lobby after sneaking out of the top-floor residence and taking the elevator down. She carried the heels and held up the red dress to ensure she didn't step on it.

The young bellman watched her approach and stepped over to get the door.

She looked down at the ground, allowing her golden locks to cover her face as she said, "Thank you."

"Miss, are you alright?" The bellman caught a glimpse of her quickly bruising cheek as she stepped forward.

She stopped and looked up, tracks of her tears visible in her makeup. "It's my fault — nothing to worry about." She attempted a brave smile.

"Jeezus, that's not alright! Do you need anything? Should I call the police?"

Her left eye was nearly swollen shut.

She stepped in close to him, putting her hand on his shoulder; she still smelled good.

"You're very kind." She kissed his cheek and stepped back. "Cute, too." She met a cab outside and was never seen there again.

High above, Terry Kinkade rolled over and took notice of the missing hooker. He shrugged his shoulder and drifted back to sleep. There had been complaints before, and none had ever led to anything. One time an officer had taken him in for questioning before BB Kinkade had been able to make some calls for his son. Turned out to be that officer's last day on the job.

7

Gordan looked out the window of the jumbo jet. He could have been coming in for a landing anywhere in the American southwest, but it was the Athens International Airport that the jet was currently dropping down upon.

The pilot was fighting strong winds and the giant jet's stall speed as he tried to bring the airship softly to the earth again. They bounced once before taxiing smoothly to the gate. Gordan waited for nearly everyone to get off before he rose to grab his duffle bag from the overhead, and then he nodded at the flight attendant as he deplaned.

The human fireplug that was Alex Giannopoulos was waiting impatiently outside the arrivals area. He was nearly five inches shorter than Hudde but maybe outweighed him by ten pounds. He wore a tight dark t-shirt tucked into dark slacks; a dark-gray jacket covered his personal firearm.

He clapped his hands together when he saw Gordan and slapped him hard on the shoulder.

"Tell me, this is the vacation you always promised, yeah?"

Gordan squeezed that thick, hairy neck. "No, my friend, I'm afraid it's all business, although my uncle has no idea where I am at the moment."

Giannopoulos shook his head. "Ah, this is no good. Why did you come so far?"

Gordan put his arm around the broad back of the shorter man, and they headed down a row of vehicles. "Find me some good food, and I'll tell you why I have come so far. I need your knowledge of the history here; maybe you can get some info from your agency without anyone paying any attention."

They stopped at a tiny Fiat, and Giannopoulos opened the door.

"You're kidding me!" Gordan wondered if the two of them would fit.

"Oh, you Americans! This is what austerity looks like to the National Intelligence Service." He smiled broadly and walked around to get behind the wheel.

Gordan cleared his throat and reached up to check to see how much clearance he had between the top of his head and the roof of the small car. "Mary Johnson met and married Andrei Crewbon at college in America. Then they came here in the late sixties or early seventies. Their son, Victor, you know as the President's Chief of Staff. I'd love to see the birth certificate, maybe the marriage certificate. Where did they live, and who did they associate with? And, maybe most important, what can we find out about the first fifteen years of young Victor?"

Giannopoulos reached over and placed a meaty paw onto Gordan's forearm. "Everyone knows that Andrei was deeply involved in the socialist coup we experienced in the late sixties. Give me two days, and you will know everything. Until then, relax, eat too much, and maybe chase the women." He grinned wide.

The tiny wheels squealed as the small car pulled into a restaurant parking lot. Giannopoulos grinned. "This will be so good!"

■ ■ ■

At a cheap motel just off I-20 near Abilene, Texas, five men split up into two rooms. The white floral van was at the farthest reaches of the parking lot but still visible from the room's windows.

They all met in Bob's room, where he spread a road map out onto the small table there. Bob showed the men where the motel was on the map and then placed an "X" on the map about five miles away from them, indicating the home of Navy SEAL Jim Foster and his family.

Bob scratched his nose and looked into the faces of the other men. "Our target lives in a small, brick ranch home. The house runs east to west, facing to the south, where the street is."

Bob reached down and placed a number "1" just west of the home out on the street. "From this location, you will be able to see the front and west side of the home. Also the van would not be visible from the other homes on the street."

Each of the men nodded an acknowledgment.

Bob placed a "2" on the east side of the house. "Here you would be visible from the house." He put a dot on the map. "But you would still see the front of the house and be off the road safely."

Bob walked over and looked out the window. "We must not violate any laws or come under any scrutiny. Once we are done here, we must begin our original plan. By tomorrow night, we must be moving. Allah be praised."

Bob pointed at Andy. "Come with me. We will take the first shift until dark. Then we will return and allow Eddy and Dan to watch until morning."

They grabbed a couple bottles of water and headed out into the early afternoon; at 67 degrees, it would be very comfortable.

The road dipped and "S" turned, dipping again just past the Foster house as the van crested the next small rise. The Foster ranch was in perfect view. Bob pulled off the road into the scrub until all the wheels were well off the road. Bob imagined that only the top third of the van would be visible from the home — *if* they bothered to look.

■ ■ ■

Josie Foster turned with a plastic cup in hand and filled it with cool water at the sink. She looked in on Jim, lying in his favorite chair in the living room just off the dining room.

She shook her head. *This has to change*, she thought. Jim had never come home like this before, and she was beyond worried at this point.

She took the small cup to her three-year-old son, who was playing quietly on the floor with some blocks. Then she turned the chain on the blinds so that a little extra light came through the patio doors. The dog raised his yellow head to see if they were going outside but set it back down when Josie walked quietly over to her husband.

She knelt down next to him, placing a hand on his chest and her chin on his arm. "Jim, you know that I don't want to know everything about war and the things you've done or seen — we've talked about all this many times. I may not be able to handle it. We've talked a lot, and I knew who and what you were when we married. But Jim, look over there — you have a son. He needs you; he needs his dad, and I need my husband back!" She smiled through the tears and then buried her head in his shoulder.

He pushed her forehead so that she had to look up, into his face, "Josie, I don't want to do this, whatever this is, but part of it is me reliving that mission over and over, seeing my friends killed." His eyes went blurry like he no longer was focusing on her.

"You and I are never going over to grill with Steve-O or Smithy and their wives and kids. I'm the 'lucky' guy who made it home, but did you know that it wasn't a rescue mission that saved me? I was getting dragged around and beaten the shit out of for days, and then one guy with a lot of luck saved me! He found me accidently! Can you imagine if that hadn't happened? The last memory of me would have been seeing me beheaded like some of them other fellas right there on the TV." Jim eyes went back out of focus and never left the wall behind her.

Josie fought the urge to break down in tears, completely losing it with this new information. She was strong, and she had to have her husband back.

She grabbed his face with both her hands and leaned in close to whisper to him.

"Jim, I need to get some groceries, okay? I need you to really look after our boy. Jesse needs you!"

He barely acknowledged her.

"Jim, we didn't celebrate your return this time, like we always have. You are going to grill some steaks, and I am going to have a bath and get all dolled up. You think you can make me scream like you used to? I'll give you extra points if we wake the neighbors!"

That got a reaction. He sat up and reached over, taking her head in the back of his hand.

"I'm sorry, Josie; I don't want to feel like this — I really don't! Don't worry. I got Jesse. You go get us those steaks and some beer. Tomorrow night, we'll celebrate like we used to."

She nodded and then turned to go to the bedroom and change; he reached back and slapped her behind enough to sting a little before she got out of range.

She yelped and turned back to him.

"The neighbors are like a mile away, you know," he reminded her.

She smiled and shook her smarting butt a little extra on the way to the bedroom. "I guess you have a real challenge, then, don't you?" she said over her shoulder.

Jim Foster stretched and shook the cobwebs from his head. He knew what was really bothering him, but he didn't dare tell her what he had been thinking.

She called out from the bedroom: "You know, a shower might do you some good, too. You're getting a bit ripe!"

He smiled — that was funny. Jesse laughed, too, throwing a plastic block into the air. No one was going to the door or the pantry, so the dog ignored everyone.

She didn't give the white van off to the side of the road a single thought as she sped out to pick up food. She was deep in thought about how she was going to keep her husband home and happy.

■ ■ ■

Gordan Hudde never relaxed; he sipped his espresso at the open-air deli, watching and taking note of everything around him. The weather was perfect, the tourists fun to watch, but Gordan was impatient.

Alex Giannopoulos approached with his own china cup, taking the seat next to Hudde.

"After that thing a few years ago, I would think you'd be more apt to be on time?"

Alex spread his hands wide. "Ah, but then, if I were on time, how would the great Gordan Hudde become the hero?" He accentuated the thought by turning his outstretched arms palms up in question.

Gordan frowned. "I almost got killed that day, you silly bastard!"

Alex took a sip of his coffee. "My men still talk about the American Devil!"

Gordan shook his head. "Tell me you have found something that can help."

Alex reached behind him and under his light jacket, pulling a manila folder from his belt line. "Here you go. Aeneas Crewbon, Victor's grandfather, started a small import/export business. Then, after World War II, this small business booms. At the same time, America has become important, so Aeneas sends his boy, Victor's father, Andrei, to America to learn everything they know."

Alex held up a finger.

"When that father returns from America to help his own papa? Mary Johnson is with him. Have you heard of the group PASOK?" He waved off a confused look from Gordan. "This is our Socialist movement from the seventies. The two of them become pretty tight with the founder of the movement. Now this is where it becomes difficult to follow. The two marry, that's in '72, and they immediately move to Iskenderun, Turkey; Aeneas had a subsidiary there. In '76, they notify both our embassies of the foreign birth of the son, Victor, but then, as you will see, the birth certificate says the birth occurred in '68, and both Mary and Andrei were in Greece that year. We have found no such birth."

Hudde sat back and started pulling at his beard.

Alex continued. "Exactly! What kind of thing is this? In 1980, Mary and Andrei show up in America with a sixteen-year-old

Victor, but where did he come from? Adopted in Turkey, you might say, but there are no Muslim orphanages. Of this I'm sure you are aware. You came for information to answer questions, and I can only give you more of a mystery."

Hudde continued to pull down on his beard. He stared a hole in the manila envelope that Alex had brought him.

"You think I'd be able to find anything in Turkey?" Gordan now looked up at Alex Giannopoulos, his brows furrowed.

Alex pointed into the sky with one finger. "This is exactly what I would do!"

"Victor Crewbon. I always thought he was another pain-in-the-ass Greek. Now, he may be Muslim?"

Alex smiled at the ribbing. "*This* pain-in-the-ass Greek has a boat waiting for you. But you must promise me that you will return one day and fill me in."

Gordan made sure that he slapped Alex a bit too hard on the back as he led him away to the waiting ship. "Thank you, my friend. You *did* help — but you still owe me, I think."

When he saw the small fishing boat that he would be riding in, Gordan turned to Alex. "Yeah — you still owe me."

"Short notice, my friend." Alex turned and walked off the pier; Gordan could hear him chuckling.

8

Josie Foster stood at the sink, finishing up the dishes. If the flood-lights had been on, she would have been able to look out the window in front of her to see their own back yard. Instead, she could see her reflection and that of the kitchen and into the den, where her husband now played on the floor with their son.

The steaks had been done perfectly over the charcoal grill out-side — and delicious, too. Jim had already been much more atten-tive with them than he had been over the last few weeks; it felt like he was coming back to them.

She smiled, thinking about the two of them maybe trying for a baby brother or sister for Jesse and the chances that their lives might grow beyond the military; she hadn't dared to say out loud to Jim what she had been praying for.

She put the last plate into the drainer and pulled the plug from the now-lukewarm water. After rinsing the last of the soapsuds from the sink and drying her hands on the towel, she turned to her two men.

She walked over to where Jim was sitting on the floor with Jesse, now just a little older than three. The two were playing with the colorful blocks that snapped together and hurt so much when you stepped on them in bare feet.

She ran her hands through Jim's hair, and he allowed his head to rest against the outside of her thigh as his hand squeezed her calf on her opposite leg.

"You, sir, are not done. I am going to go get ready. You are going to make sure Jesse is put to bed. Then I have a new outfit to ask your opinion on."

"Oh, really?" Jim smiled up at her as he allowed his hand to snake up her denim-covered leg, across her behind, and up under the back of her shirt to caress the bare skin on her back.

"Oh, no — not yet!" She wagged a finger at him and headed toward the bathroom; she grabbed the half-full wine bottle as she went by.

"Hooyah, master chief!" he called out to her.

Josie took a swig straight from the bottle and locked the bathroom door behind her. She opened her cabinets and began to look over all the lotions and concoctions that she had purchased at one time or another.

Making the proper selections, she started water in the tub, pouring a light-blue liquid into the stream of warm water; it began to fill and foam at the same time.

She lit two candles, took another swig of wine, and set the bottle down where she could reach it while in the tub, and then she unwrapped a new razor, setting it on top of the bar of soap. The radio was always set to the same country-western station, and she turned it down low. She stepped into the tub and slid slowly down into the soapy warm water, allowing it to relax her. At five foot three inches, she could get lost in this tub, but Jim never took a bath because his long lanky, body only fit half of him at a time.

She reached for the bottle and carefully pulled it up for another drink. It felt strange as the cool liquid went down into her as she was surrounded by the warm water. She allowed her head to fall back, where she'd folded a towel as a pillow to protect against the tile. Maybe she even fell asleep for a few minutes until she heard Jim stomp down the hallway — probably with little Jesse over his shoulder, getting him ready to go to bed.

Then she took the razor and began to preen. She just wanted to be a woman for the rest of the night; she wanted to feel good and make her husband want her. When she stood to put lotion all over, she was smooth from her neck to her toes. She felt a bit naughty — she had never shaved completely before, and it added to her own excitement.

She teased her hair so that it looked wild and full, and then she peeked out into the hall to make sure that Jim was back out in the living room. She tiptoed naked down the hall into their bedroom, where she pulled out the tiny little panties and the cream-colored baby doll. She slipped the satin outfit on, admiring how her nipples were visible through the thin, silky fabric.

She slipped on her girly-girl fuzzy slippers with the kitten heel and "clickety-clacked" down the hall until she made it to the doorway to the den, where Jim was back in front of the TV, drinking a beer.

She leaned against the wall and slid one hand up the frame as high as she could reach, while bending one knee until her heel nearly touched her behind.

"What do you think, handsome?"

He set down his beer and stood up, letting out a wolf whistle as he did.

"Lady, you can't be here. My wife could come back home any second."

She did her best runway walk behind the couch just out of his reach, and she leaned against the lunch counter, looking back at him over her shoulder.

"Too bad you're married. I bet a big military man like yourself could really use a date!" She allowed her hips to alternately take her weight, and she pouted, pursing her bright-red lips.

Jim stepped into and then over the sofa quicker than she thought he could move. She shrieked and tried to run as he reached for her. His big, rough hands actually felt good against her soft, smooth skin, and she giggled and pretended to fight as he picked her up and brought her back around to the right side of the couch.

"Mister — please! What about your wife!" She laughed until he grabbed a handful of her hair and began to bite and tease her neck.

His lovemaking was physical and needy, maybe a bit too quick, but she forgave him under the circumstances.

After, they both fell asleep on the floor near the couch, the TV flickering as they dreamt.

■ ■ ■

It was nearing 2:00 am, and Bob was getting anxious; there was still a light on in the front of the house. He shook his head and then climbed into the back of the van.

Bob motioned, and the men opened the locker.

Inside were an assortment of weapons, Bob ignored the rifles and pulled out a small handgun. He checked it and then added a few drops of gun oil. He manipulated the action several times, feeling it glide easily, and then he screwed a silencer onto the barrel. He removed the empty magazine and checked the spring. He filled it with the special low-velocity rounds and handed both over to Dan, who locked and loaded the gun, nodding at Bob.

Reaching back into the box, Bob selected two nine-inch crowbars. Sliding one into his own belt, he gave the other to Eddy.

Bob, Dan, and Chuck were going to go around to the back to see if they could gain access to a back door, while Eddy and Andy were tasked to kick in the front doors once they heard any commotion inside.

They all climbed out of the van. Taking the magnetic signs off, they huddled one last time.

Bob raised his finger and wagged it. "This morning, we are the first strike against the great Satan!"

A hushed but excited "*Allahu Akbar*" was returned by his men.

Bob reminded his men one last time, "We must have the male answer questions; the others, ultimately, do not matter."

His men nodded, and they looked back over to the Foster house. Seeing that the lights were now all off, Bob nodded — they all knew what had to be done.

■ ■ ■

Hudde looked around the small galley of the bucking fishing trawler that he had been on for nearly twelve hours. There was nothing that looked even remotely like a lifejacket. The thunder was probably roaring, but he couldn't hear it over the sound of the waves — twice as high as the craft — throwing this boat around. No rollercoaster he had ever been on could hold a candle to this ride.

At first, he took solace in the fact that he wasn't seasick. It now appeared that throwing himself out of all kinds of aircraft was completely reasonable compared to this. Fuck the ocean, fuck the seas, fuck fish, and fuck everything related to deep waters.

When calm seas came with the morning light, Hudde was thankful to step onto land, even if it was Izmir, Turkey. He smiled a bit sheepishly at the grinning fishermen, slung his ruck over his shoulder, and headed out to find the train station.

■ ■ ■

Josie awoke when her head slid off Jim's chest; it was nearly two in the morning, and she shook him awake.

"Come on, honey. Let's go to bed." She reached across him to grab her panties and kissed his chin.

"Okay, Josie. Right behind you." He playfully slapped her bare behind as she stepped away.

She padded on soft bare feet into the bedroom, where the sheets felt cold when she slid in between them.

She wondered if he would want her again. She hoped so, but the slowly warming sheets caused her to fall back into a deep sleep.

Jim sat up and turned off the TV; he slid on his Navy-emblazoned sweatpants and went into the kitchen to brew a fresh pot of coffee. That way, in the morning, they could just pour and nuke a pretty fresh cup.

He tip-toed into the bedroom to check on Josie; she was snoring a little. One shapely leg stuck out from under the sheet, and he wondered if he could wake her. He decided that he should let her sleep, covered her, and kissed her temple before heading back to the kitchen.

Screw it, he thought and poured himself a steaming cup of joe.

He carried the mug over to his chair and plopped down, thinking. He realized that what was bothering him so much was not that he didn't know what to do next, but it was how he was going to tell Josie.

He knew he had nothing to prove to himself, but he needed to support the remaining team members. He needed to extract some revenge for the fallen.

He hated thinking that he would disappoint his wife, but maybe just one last tour.

■ ■ ■

Outside the Foster home, two shadowy figures had made it to the end of the driveway, starting to creep up toward the front door. Once there, they stepped up under the small overhang and waited quietly.

Three men had made it past the back of the ranch house and into a small stand of mesquite and ash trees. Dan had the Makarov ready in his right hand and the small steak in his left.

Bob nodded at Chuck, and he sprinted across the open space, past the plastic swing set up against the back of the house, kneeling near the gray metal air conditioning unit. Bob stood up from his crouch before a metal-on-metal noise stopped him in his tracks, and he knelt back down, one hand leaning against a small tree.

■ ■ ■

Jim Foster realized he may have fallen asleep in the chair but his lab, Fubar, was dancing in front of him like she needed to go out.

He smiled and rubbed her head. "Okay, sweetie. I'll get you out of here."

He stood and stretched before heading to the drapes at the sliding glass doors. He pushed the drapes aside just enough to flip the latch to the heavier glass door, and he pulled it back enough to slip his hand through and also unlock the screen door. Then he pushed them both to his left at the same time. Fubar began pushing her head through well before it was wide enough, and she burst out into the night as soon as she could wiggle through.

Josie would be angry if she saw Jim do this without first opening the curtains, but Jim did this all the time. Just like the ongoing argument about toilet seats, it just happened — Josie argued that, soon, it would be two against one! He didn't close the door. He would just wait until Fubar came back in; besides, the screeching noise the door made might wake the kid if he had to repeat it two extra times.

Jim turned and walked back to his chair. Fubar barked once, but that was it. She'd probably seen some other critter out in the night. Jim hoped it wasn't a skunk...or a snake.

■ ■ ■

The dog ran right at Bob, hiding in the trees. The motion-activated floodlights at the center of the house flipped on, lighting up the backyard like it was high noon. Bob held the crowbar high, waiting. Dan waved the meat, hoping that the smell would get the dog's attention. It worked, and the lab ran straight to Dan, now dangling the meat, tempting the dog closer.

She barked once and then sat down, waiting for a treat. Dan dropped the meat, and, as the dog leaned forward to get the reward, she was shot in the top of the head. She died instantly.

The noise was not all that loud, but they froze in the manufactured daylight.

No one came to the window, so Bob and Chuck ran across the open yard to the cooling units as Chuck began walking toward the sliding glass doors, hugging the wall.

Dan looked down and saw that the spent cartridge was stuck in the chamber of the small gun. He needed to manually remove it and then jack a new round into the breech by pulling back on the slide and then allowing the mechanism to spring forward.

■ ■ ■

Jim sat in the chair with both hands on top of his head, thumbs against each temple, rubbing. He opened his eyes briefly to reach for his coffee mug when he looked at the drapes and observed the silhouettes of multiple men moving across the sheer fabric.

He jumped up from his chair. *Damn!* His weapons were locked away in a safe in the back bedroom to keep his child away from danger! Now he looked around quickly for something he could use but saw nothing.

9

The rocking motion of the train put Gordan Hudde in a near trance-like state. The bogus identification that Alex Giannopoulos had given him worked without any questions. It was not uncommon to have dual citizenship in Greece and Turkey.

Gordan kept to himself; he could mutter some acceptable Pashto that had helped in Afghanistan. But even with the wide mix of all kinds of people, it was not widely spoken in Turkey.

He was second-guessing this whirlwind tour. What if the meeting with Crewbon and Kinkade was just a back-channel "eyes only" mission — known and fully accepted by the President?

Was this a total waste of time? What did he hope to find out? Talk about grasping at straws. But he kept going back to the position that there was no way the President's Chief of Staff would be at that meeting in the mountains of Iraq, and that well-timed attack on a hidden SEAL team... it couldn't be a coincidence.

A guy like Kinkade, sure. Maybe an embedded Special Forces team, yeah, but not the Chief of Staff at the meeting. Gordan

tugged down on his beard and shook his head. Absolutely no fucking way.

Gordan's train ride would take him to Iskenderun, a small
coastal village wedged between mountains and the Mediterranean,
where the Crewbon grandfather once allowed his son to run the
branch of his import/export empire.

■ ■ ■

Chuck reached over and grasped the screen door, sliding it further
open so he could fit through. The heavier glass door screeched as
it slid, loud in the otherwise quiet night air.

As soon as he started forward, a foot came out of the drapes,
striking Chuck firmly in the sternum. Chuck lost all the air in his
lungs and stumbled backwards, falling and striking the back of his
head on the concrete bench. The heavy outdoor patio furniture
had been purchased to ensure that the violent winds from Texas
storms didn't send their furniture flying into cow pastures nearby.

Chuck was totally taken by surprise, and he died there for this
mistake.

Dan got caught up in the drapes trying to bring the handgun
up to aim. Jim Foster grabbed the intruder's wrist, pulling him
further into the house and twisting his arm up, over, and down.
He slammed Dan into the doorframe and put tremendous pressure on his elbow.

"Who the fuck are you?" Jim screamed into the intruder's ear.

Hearing the commotion inside, Eddy and Andy crashed
through the front door. Momentarily confused by the twisting and
turning bodies spun into the drapes, the two men stood near the
hallway going back into the home.

Dan pushed off the wall and the two men fell toward the floor. He tried to turn the gun toward the American, and, while the gun went off, there was nothing that proved the American had been hit.

Bob came into the kitchen, yanking the half-torn drapes from the broken rods hanging from the wall brackets. He stepped over Dan and struck Jim Foster in the right temple with enough force to knock him unconscious. Bob looked over to see Andy leaning against the wall, bent at the waist and holding a rapidly spreading dark spot under his hand.

Bob pointed at Eddy. "Get back there now," he said, and he pointed down the hallway.

A small child startled Eddy as he made his way down the hall, and Eddy kicked him in the chest, sending him flying backwards. The boy's chest caved in from the force of the heavy, steel-toed boots and Eddy's superior size. Jesse Foster took only two or three more ragged breaths before he died in the hallway.

Eddy charged into the master bedroom, where Josie Foster was frantically trying to open the safe. The battery-operated pad on the safe beeped to notify her that she had entered the incorrect password.

She turned, saw Eddy, and screamed. He had to reach across the corner of the bed, but his punch landed on her temple, and she crumpled down where she was standing.

When she came back to consciousness, she had been tied up and was now lying on her back on the bed she shared with Jim. She was shaking in fear because she did not know what had happened to her son or Jim.

A dark, bearded man stood over her. His knife flashed in what little light came out from the bathroom nightlight, and Eddy smiled at her as the blade passed back and forth across her line of vision.

Jim Foster regained consciousness and found himself zip-tied to one of the kitchen chairs. He didn't pick up his head but allowed it to dangle, as if he were still sleeping. The chair wasn't designed for this, but he would not be able to get free without a lot of noise, bringing attention to himself. He decided to fully open his eyes and look around at whatever had befallen him.

Bob walked over and picked up the handgun lying on the floor. He needed to clear the blockage to chamber another round. He stepped back in front of the Navy SEAL and leaned down to look into the man's eyes. They seemed clear enough.

"We shall start. Understand this, Mr. Jim Foster. We have your family. You are powerless to stop us. Do not test our will, or your family will die in needless pain."

He continued to look into the SEAL's eyes. "Are you understanding me?"

Foster knew what he would do if he were back in the Middle East, but having these men here in his home, his wife and infant child at risk, he didn't know what to do.

Bob now felt free to speak in his native tongue. He called out to his brother in the back of the house, "Mustapha, let this spawn of evil hear his woman scream!"

Eddy leaned into Josie's ear and whispered that she shouldn't move or he may accidentally cut her. He waved the knife again as he cut the rope and pulled the washcloth from her mouth.

He flipped her over easily so that she lay on her belly, hands under her. He cut the strap of cloth that held the small triangular patches of her panties together, and he roughly pulled them off.

"Wait — No!" she screamed, and then Eddy pushed the back of her head down, her face sinking down into the mattress.

Eddy admired her taut bottom and soft skin, but she seemed dangerously thin; he thought she would not make a good child bearer. She would not have been comforted by his thought that he would rather abuse her dead son's body.

Jim started to strain against the wood and plastic, but Bob placed the small semi-auto to his temple.

"You fought bravely. You and your family can die quickly, or we can keep them alive for days until, we tire of them."

Foster talked through clenched teeth. "What do you want?"

"We need to know who you told about your last mission. Tell me that, and you will go quickly." Bob stood tall now over his enemy.

Foster shook his head. "I don't know anything, so I couldn't tell anyone anything."

Bob walked over to the hallway and called back to Eddy, this time in English. "I guess he does not know who we are. Again, please."

Eddy allowed Josie to gather her breath. Then he pulled her legs over the side of the bed. He forced himself between her legs so that his groin was positioned behind her. Then he pulled back on her head until he could whisper into her ear.

"After I take your son, we will take turns on you till you die."

Josie let out a blood-curdling scream. When she started to take a breath, Eddy returned her face into the mattress.

"No!" Jim Foster bellowed. The arm on one side of the chair splintered with his rage. Bob struck him hard enough with the steel bar to break his collarbone, sending him backwards onto the floor, fighting to stay conscious, three limbs still tied to the broken chair.

"One more mistake, and we kill your son. The second one, we will drag your wife out here and rape her on her boy's corpse." Bob sneered.

Jim Foster gave up; he could fight to the death but couldn't dare think about his wife and son.

"I saw two Americans in the mountains, but I didn't put it in a report; I swear it."

Bob stood over the top of Foster. "This is something we already knew, and this is good. Now, who did you tell?"

"I...I..." Foster still struggled to come to grips with what was happening here in his own country, in his own home.

"We already know. We are just making sure what we have is correct. Please save your family more pain." Bob shook his head.

"I only told one person."

Bob got down on one knee. "Yes?"

"A CIA agent by the name of Gordan Hudde. He's the only one...please..."

"The man that saved you?" Bob stood again. "Why just him?"

"I can't really tell you...his reputation, I guess. I knew he would not tell anyone." Foster put his head back, totally broken.

Bob shot him in the temple and then swore. "This piece of shit!" The semi-expended brass shell was jammed in the mechanism.

Andy had slipped into a seated position near the hallway to the bedrooms. Bob walked over to look at the wound, and he told Dan to get the van, back it into the driveway, and bring in a five-gallon can of gas when he returned. Bob knelt, putting his hand on Andy's head as he spoke.

"My brother, our battle will continue, thanks to your help. *Allahu Akbar.*" He put the small-caliber gun in Andy's right eye and pulled the trigger. Bob sighed audibly when he had to jack another round into the chamber. He removed the magazine to check to see if the spring's tension had failed. He shook his head and dropped the gun back into his pocket.

Bob peeked into each door before getting to the master bed-room. He inspected the attractive woman in the frilly clothing. "It is too bad we do not have the time to fully appreciate this woman."

Eddy took the pressure off her head, and she gasped for air. "What... what did you do to my husband?"

"The same thing we will do to all our enemies." Bob then reached over for Eddy's knife to cut her throat. Her bladder emp-tied, and both men stepped away as she wriggled and died.

They met Dan as he came in the broken front door with the gas can. Bob took the can and told his two remaining fighters to drag their brother back into the house from the back patio. Bob finished pouring the gas around the house as the other two fin-ished getting Chuck into the kitchen.

Bob looked at Dan. "Once we get into the van, you stand in the door and start a fire, and then we will continue with our mission."

Bob climbed into the driver's seat and started the van. Eddy opened the rear doors but then took the passenger seat. Dan ran and jumped into the back, closing the doors of the van at the same time.

As they sped away from the home, Dan looked out the back window; each time the house came into view, the fire appeared larger and larger. Dan was sad that the workload would now have to be carried by fewer men, but he was happy to have some kind of seat now.

10

Gordan stepped out from the train into the mid-morning air that had not yet been touched by the sun, still hidden by the mountain to the east. In fact, Gordan thought that the town may not get sun until after lunch. Gordan's skin crawled, and he wondered if it was the cool mountain air rushing down from the peaks or if *someone had walked over his grave.*

He felt a bit exhausted from the travel; the boat trip alone nearly destroyed his nerves. His mind kept examining the weaknesses of his thought process, and he feared he was wasting time.

So close to Lebanon, Syria, and Iraq, the city of Iskenderun was filled with all kinds of people. While many would easily be typecast as the heavy in any spy movie, there were also tourists and other visitors here to check out the port area, with its many strange antique dealers and specialty shops.

Gordan stepped into the building that once held the Aeneas Crewbon business. A young dark man sipped tea from a fine white bone china cup decorated with blue dragons. The long, slim glass case also acted as the desk for the register. Gordan couldn't discern exactly what was being sold here; it could have been a large pawn shop, judging from the mixture of wares on display.

The young man nodded and fired off something that Gordan did not understand, something with a Russian-sounding "*da*" at the end.

Gordan shook his head and tried his Pashto, getting the same response from the young man.

"Fuck," Gordan said as he looked around the shop.

"Oh, English," the young man said behind him.

Gordan turned back. "Yeah — any chance that someone here remembers the Crewbon business that used to be here?"

"I've heard of them, but nobody who worked for them is still working here now." He stared at Gordan, waiting to see if there was anything more.

Gordan grabbed his beard and pulled down as he realized his fears. This had been a worthless trip. He turned away, saying, "Thanks" over his shoulder.

"Wait," the kid called out after him.

"There is an old guy who hangs out around here most of the time. Hair all white, no teeth, and a big turban."

Gordan turned back. "Yes?"

"Well, if anyone knows anything about those days, it's him." The young man shrugged.

Gordan nodded. "Okay, then — better than nothing. Thanks," and he turned back outdoors, the small bells over the door ringing as the door pivoted.

Gordan began walking through the small stores and fish markets along the dock area, looking for a man who fit the description. Just as his stomach began to demand lunch, he felt like he'd found him. He had small, bony arms with brown-parchment skin covering them. The turban was so large, it looked as if the scrawny neck should not be able to hold it up.

Gordan was again stifled by an inability to speak with the area elder. Through sign language, he was able to get the man to begin to follow him back toward the old Crewbon business. With the building in sight, the old man sat down on an old wooden barrel outside another shop and put up his hand up while shaking his head.

Gordan pleaded and pointed at the shopfront, but the man would just look down Gordan's arm to his pointing finger and shake his head.

Gordan gave him the same hand gestures that he would have given a dog to "sit" and "stay" and then pointed back and forth between himself and the shop.

The old man stared back blankly.

Oh, well. The guy can't get too far, Gordan thought and took off back to the Crewbon shop.

The young man behind the counter showed no sign of recognition as Gordan ran back into the shop, the bells clanging.

"Hey, I think I found the guy," Gordan explained. "If that's him down there," he pointed out the door. "Could you interpret for me?"

"I'd love to help you out, but I must stay in the shop," he replied without emotion and shrugged his shoulders.

Gordan stood at the door, pointing. "I don't know why he stopped there, but, can you see him, right there?" Gordan didn't want to get so close and then walk away without a conversation, at a minimum.

No reaction.

Gordan pulled out a roll of euros. "I don't even know how much is here, but you can have it if you help."

The kid leaned over the counter and inspected Gordan's offer. "Alright, for a moment," and he began to follow.

The old man had not yet moved. The kid stopped in front of him, and they had some kind of interaction.

"Ask him if he knows anything about Aeneas or Andrei Crewbon from when they used to own that building back there," Gordan told the kid, pointing with his thumb over his shoulder.

The old man's face lit up, and Gordan took that as a good sign. He went on for a good five minutes before the kid waved him to stop.

"He knows everything, he says. Aeneas was a brilliant mind and fair trader. He was well respected by everyone who did business with him, and they came from all over the world, right to that shop back there."

"After all of that talking, I get one sentence?"

"Listen, mister. I don't know what's important, and the old man is willing to talk all day." He took a deep breath. "Anything else?"

"Yes. Please ask him about the son, Andrei. What was he like when he took over the business?"

The old man got very agitated; he shook his head and waved his hands out before him as he spoke.

"Nope, they didn't like him at all; he had no mind for business and did not get along with the other merchants. Then he sold everything once the father, Aeneas, died."

"Yeah, but they lived here for some time. What did they do, and who did they hang out with?"

The old man pointed up at the mountains behind them, the sun battling to rise up and over them. At one point, he looked left and right before speaking in a hushed tone.

"What was that about?" Gordan asked the kid.

"I don't know. The son, Andrei, and his wife used to spend a lot of time up in the mountains. There once was a group called 'The *Ghuzz*,' known for some violent acts on behalf of Islam." The kid shrugged. "I really need to get back."

"Wait! Ask him where I can find these people."

The kid looked at Gordan like he was crazy and then turned back to the old man. He turned back to Gordan. "A day's ride that way." He pointed northeast. "A village called Atiak, he thinks."

Gordan pulled the wad of bills out of his pocket; he peeled off a few bills and showed them to the kid. "Can you get a meal with this around here?"

"A few," the kid said.

Gordan nodded and handed them to the old man. Then he passed the rest to the kid. "Thank you," he said, and he got a cab to the edge of the city.

The land rose up, and Gordan walked. He was able to hitch a ride in an old farm truck that had Gordan beginning to wonder if he could walk faster than it moved up the steep incline, but it was a welcome relief. When they came upon the pass to the north that he had to take, Gordan rapped on the side of the truck, and it came to a stop, letting him out. He knew that the map made it look easy; they always did.

By the time Gordan reached the southern edge of the town he was looking for, his calves were burning. There were maybe a hundred mud and rock buildings or dwellings; a single mosque minaret rose above all at the far north of the village. There were no shops, no restaurants, and no hotels to attract anyone from the outside world. It had been a single, three-hour drive, and now Gordan was 800 years back in time.

While no one had paid him any attention in Iskenderun, everyone's head turned as Gordan began walking the main street toward the mosque. He was waiting for a scream like in the movie *The Invasion of the Body Snatchers.* There was nothing that he could do but push on. As he approached the mosque, Gordan noticed an old man sitting like some kind of sentinel on a wood-and-stone bench. As Gordan watched to see if the man moved, his mind began racing, finding negative thoughts.

What the hell did I think I was going to accomplish here? I knew before the trip I would most likely contact people hostile to the west, so why did I bother to come? Did I think I could just walk into this village and start asking about Crewbon, as I did in the shop down by the coast?

He shrugged his shoulders and walked on. Behind the mosque, the little road turned into a path, and, not long after that, it was nothing more than a game or goat trail. Gordan stopped when the trail picked through rocks along a steep cliff. He sat on a rock until he shrugged his shoulders and put the negative thoughts behind him. Regardless of his doubts, he had come this far for a reason.

He walked back down toward the town; at least now the cold wind was at his back. At the mosque, Gordan walked around the other side and stood still, watching the old man who appeared not to have moved. Gordan was now sure that Victor Crewbon was not the child of Mary and Andrei. He folded his arms and matched the old man, standing silently.

Men began to straggle out; they stood and they talked. Some glanced over at the stranger, but none approached.

Gordan began to wonder if he was going to stand in that spot all night, when the old man reached out to a child as he exited the mosque. He pulled the child close, and they spoke. Then the boy approached Gordan.

The boy spoke, and Gordan did not understand. The boy pointed back at the old man; Gordan took it as an opportunity to approach.

Gordan placed his right hand on his heart and bowed. "Peace be upon you, Imam." He prayed the old man would understand.

The old man did not look up. "Strangers often find the road to our village difficult and dangerous."

Gordan knew that this moment was the one he was hoping, for "to obtain the truth, we must be willing to walk a dangerous path."

The old man nodded.

Gordan continued, "In my land, our people have been made promises from one we do not know. In confidence, he has shared the place of his birth for me to go out to find the truth."

"Who is this man?" the Imam asked.

"This man is not trusted by many of our wise men, as he is seated to the right of the great Satan."

The old man looked up for the first time. He studied Gordan for what seemed a long time, and Gordan spoke no more.

"Wait," the old man finally said. Getting up, he shuffled inside.

Gordan had been in situations like this before, where one part of his mind told him to run, while another forced him to stand his ground. Would the Imam return with men to try to take him captive, maybe turn him into the next Internet beheading?

Thirty minutes later, Gordan set down his ruck and pulled out a heavy sweater. Sixty minutes later, he decided that there was not going to be men rushing out of the darkness surrounding him. And then the old man shuffled out; he gestured for Gordan to follow and went back inside.

Gordan followed, and the old man stopped at a lit candle on a small table. He picked up an old black-and-white photo and held it out for Gordan to take.

Gordan looked at the old photo of what appeared to be this very mosque, many years ago, with an adult male whose back was to the camera and who was surrounded by many boys. Their hands were all held high over their heads, as if the camera had caught some moment of elation.

Gordan felt he'd looked at the photo long enough. "Yes?"

"If the man you speak of is in this photo, I will tell you what I know." The old man folded his arms; done.

How the fuck could he pick out Crewbon as a kid?

Gordan returned his attention to the photo. Crewbon was a runt; he began to look for the littlest kid. Several of the kids' faces were not visible, as they were looking down or other arms obscured their faces. He studied the little faces, sweating now that he was out of the cold wind.

Gordan had never met this guy. He had seen him on TV, but how was he going to pick him out from a forty-five-year-old photo?

Gordan dropped his arm and looked at the old man. "What if I cannot?"

The old man's brows furrowed. "Then, be gone." He dismissed Gordan with a wave of his arm, and he reached for the photo.

Then a thought came to Gordan. He remembered a childhood friend, an Italian, who had shot up a foot taller than Gordan and for a year or two was the giant in his class. The thing was that kid had quit growing at five-foot-five. All his friends had eventually caught up and then grown larger, until his Italian friend was one of the shortest in his class.

Gordan pulled the photo away from the old man, now looking at the bigger kids. There he was, face looking up to the heavens, hands high above head, the big gash across his left eyebrow.

Gordan slapped the photo down onto the table, placing his index finger onto the face he thought he recognized. "Here is the man we are concerned with."

The old man's gaze followed from Gordan's fingertip up to his face. "The *Mahdi* raises. *Allahu Akbar!*"

Gordan kept tapping the face of young Victor Crewbon with his finger. "Tell me, if this man is truly of us, how then does he sit at the table with the great Satan?"

The old Imam shook his head. "This one will not be deterred; his reverence to Muhammad and Allah should not be questioned, no matter where he sits. Go back and tell your people that."

The old man returned Gordan's attention to the photo. He reached out and removed Gordan's finger from the likeness of Crewbon and pointed a withered and bony finger at the adult in the photo.

"Me," he stated. "I taught him the way of *jihad*, and I will live to see the great Caliphate. He will convert the world to the teachings of Muhammad, blessing be upon him."

"Well, then," Gordan started. "May Allah heap blessing upon you."

"Oh, he has. I will live to see the great *Mahdi* bring judgment to the world."

Gordan didn't show it, but a shiver went up his spine. He vowed to himself that this old man would never live to see that day.

"My people thank you. *Allahu Akbar.*" He turned once to look back and saw the old man's toothless grin.

A three-hour drive is a long walk. Gordan did not sleep, and he did not start back down the mountain. He needed to get back to the States and pull some strings there. He had seen *The Manchurian Candidate*. Now he was worried that Victor Crewbon was the Manchurian Advisor. The fastest way back was to get to the International airport in Aleppo, Syria, so Gordan headed further up and inland.

Gordan guessed he could get a flight to France and then be in New York by what would be late tomorrow night. He walked until he caught a ride in another old truck bed, this time with a few chickens in wooden crates. Gordan's mind drifted while he caught some uneasy sleep. *Does Dubois know?* Then almost immediately, Gordan thought, *How could he not? They've been joined at the hip since college.*

11

The morning security briefing over, Dubois was talking to his press secretary about possibly making a statement about the loss of a Navy SEAL, a hero who had lived in Texas.

Victor Crewbon interrupted. "Do you think this is wise, sir? There is so little information. For all we know, it was a robbery gone wrong; there is no need to get everyone speculating on nationality or if it was a terrorist attack or not."

Dubois paced several moments and turned to his secretary. "How about you send a personal note to his command with our deepest regrets, and then we will wait for additional facts."

The oval office door closed behind the press secretary, and Crewbon sat making himself comfortable, satisfied with how things were proceeding.

"Imagine, Lemme. Two young men sharing big dreams in college, talking crazy about revolution and leading the people, and now look at what you have accomplished."

Dubois sat behind the "Resolute Desk," leaning back, enjoying the adulation from his advisor.

"You get the Israelis to sign this deal, you'll win the election easily," Crewbon continued. "And two out of the next four years you can do anything you want. Hell, you may earn a democrat congress and the honeymoon will continue for the entire four years. Imagine what you could accomplish!"

Dubois had his eyes closed and his head back, taking in the thought, nodding slowly.

Crewbon now leaned onto the front of the desk. "Eliminating the second amendment, real single-payer healthcare, and borders ignored. Lemme, your party will win elections for the next fifty years." Crewbon sat back, satisfied by the glow coming from Dubois's face.

The President should have been a bit concerned over the phrase "your party," but he was too busy thinking about the possibilities that his face would be added to Mt. Rushmore.

Suddenly Dubois sat up, eyes wide. Now he leaned onto his desk and spoke in an excited, hushed tone. "Victor, imagine, as my time here comes to an end, maybe with the proper disturbance or issue with our election, and I remain in office indefinitely!" He clapped his hands once and allowed them to remain out in front of him, palms up, shoulder-width apart. "Maybe I get elected president for life. Who knows? It has happened often throughout history."

Victor's sneer widened, making him squint through his right eye. "Hold on, my liege," he said sarcastically. "We must not overlook even the smallest of things that may upset our plans, but, Lemme, I do believe that what you envision could be made real."

"But, Victor, we are so close. What could go wrong?" Dubois glanced around the room while he waited for an answer.

"Well, for instance, my sources say that the CIA is trying to find out who we may have negotiated with during the past year."

Dubois's brows furrowed while he thought. Then he shrugged his shoulders. "So?"

"Mr. President." Crewbon suddenly sounded tired. "We have done the exact opposite of everything you said to get elected. We have negotiated with terrorists, we have given our "enemies" (he made quote marks in the air) concessions that could have gotten you impeached, for crying out loud!"

Crewbon now stood and rubbed his left eyebrow. "Even with the most duplicitous news agencies covering you, you wouldn't survive to see your next election."

Dubois opened the deep side drawer and pulled out the antacid. Going from jubilant to despondent in just minutes was causing the back of his throat to burn.

"What should I do?"

Crewbon pretended to think, but this is where he'd wanted this conversation to go all along. Now, he just had to make sure that Dubois thought these were his own ideas.

"Well, maybe CIA Director Smith could share some information about this. Maybe he would see you."

"What are you talking about, 'maybe'? He works for me, doesn't he?" He didn't wait for an answer. He just pointed at Crewbon. "You make sure his ass is in that chair before the day is over."

"If that's what you wish." Victor didn't waste a moment and took this as his cue to leave the office.

Standing just outside the Oval Office door, waiting to gain entry, was the Vice President, an even bigger sap as far as Crewbon was concerned. He walked past him without even acknowledging his presence.

The Vice President knew better than to speak to Crewbon, and then he had second thoughts about whatever it was that he was waiting to speak to the President about. He did a one-eighty, heading back to his office.

12

As Gordan Hudde's flight went "feet wet" over the Atlantic, the CIA Director, Ben Smith, was pulling up a chair in the Oval Office.

Smith was a big, heavy man; his breathing was labored from the walk through the halls of the White House. He had been a two-term governor of Virginia before being selected by Dubois to be Director. Smith knew that he was a political appointee, with no law enforcement or national security in his background, and pleasing the administration was job one.

He was breathing hard from the walk, but now he was sweating from the questions that Crewbon and Dubois were asking.

"I'm sorry, Mr. President. I really do not know what investigation you are talking about." He turned in his chair to also glance back at Victor Crewbon, who was leaning against the paneled door behind him.

"Then you don't have control of your department," Crewbon suggested.

Dubois let the insult sit for a moment. "Listen, Ben. We have some very delicate negotiations going on right now. I—" he put his hand against his chest. "We… can't allow gossip or leaks to somehow drive people from the table. We are close to a greater peace in the Middle East."

"Peace?"

"You don't need to know right now, but soon. Anyway, I need you to rein in your agent Gordan Hudde. I've been told he's handling the investigation."

"Well, 'Hudde' is a name I'm familiar with. The Deputy Director uses him for the most difficult situations. He's highly decorated." Smith took a moment to glance back and forth between the two men. "But I'm unaware of an investigation at this time into any of Mr. Crewbon's travel; I'll put a stop to it immediately."

Crewbon was suddenly at his side. "Just what will you be 'putting a stop to'?"

"I assure you…"

Crewbon interrupted. "I'm not confident you could assure me of anything right now."

"Well, wait just one second…"

Dubois interrupted the Director. "Now, now. Let cooler heads prevail here. I'll tell you what, Ben. Why don't you get this Hudde fellow into your office and figure out what may or may not be going on behind your back? Then you could fill us in; let's say tomorrow afternoon."

Crewbon walked over and whispered into the President's ear. Dubois looked back at Smith. "Tomorrow at one, I will expect you back here giving me an update."

Dubois and Crewbon put their heads together and began to whisper. Crewbon looked back over at Smith. "Tomorrow at one," he said, and then he returned to his private conversation with Dubois.

Ben Smith looked about the room for a moment and then got up to leave. He felt a bit awkward not saying something, but neither of the other men stopped to look, so he turned and showed himself out.

■ ■ ■

Gordan Hudde cleared customs at JFK before using his phone to contact Deputy Director Stevens. He relayed the factual information that he had uncovered before speculating about Crewbon's parents helping to get the "Manchurian Advisor" into the White House.

"I can give you many adjectives that describe that info right now, but, unfortunately, it proves nothing. It's speculation based on very few hard facts. What I do know for a fact is that you and I are supposed to be front and center in the Director's office tomorrow morning."

"What does he want from me?"

"I'm not exactly sure, but he was agitated — I *can* tell you that. 'Straight from the President himself,' Director Smith said to me."

Hudde got into his rental for a drive back to the Virginia area. "It can't be a coincidence, right?"

"You won't know because you're still in South America. I'll get in touch after the meeting, and, by the way, I'm sorry about the Navy SEAL. It's a travesty, after the rescue and all."

"Wait — what?" Gordan waited before starting the car.

"Oh, I'm sorry. There was some kind of crime scene at the Foster residence. There were five bodies burned beyond recognition."

"What kind of crime scene?" Hudde thought his voice sounded an octave too high.

"It's just too early to know for sure."

"There were only three of them, boss. Who were the other two? This has to have something to do with his last mission. Has the fire been ruled arson?"

"I haven't heard anything else, son. I'll reach out to the local fire department and PD."

"He was the only living witness, and now he's gone. This is no coincidence. I'll bet Crewbon was behind it."

Stevens was silent, and the phone seemed to go dead. Then it crackled. "This is so thin...but there are other witnesses. I can't let you get close to Crewbon, but I don't care what happens to Kinkade. I'll cover for you as long as I can, but I need to know what the hell this is all about. You do what you have to, and don't get caught in the process. But it needs to be concrete — understand? If this is all related, you and I are up against it, right now! Hear me?"

"Loud and clear, boss. And when I find out what happened to the Fosters..."

"Agreed." The line was disconnected.

13

Terry Kinkade strode confidently from the elevator at his Four Seasons Residence. Kinkade had no sense of self-awareness. He was not liked by many, but from the way he walked the halls — head high, shoulders back — you wouldn't know it.

Gordan Hudde stepped up into his space, holding a cup of coffee in each hand.

"Jesus! Hudde, you should really wear a bell or something. Why are you sneaking around my hotel?"

"No way to treat a coworker. I even brought you a coffee. I thought we could go get some breakfast." He held the coffee up at shoulder height.

Kinkade had two inches on Hudde and used it to look down disapprovingly at Hudde's attire. "Do you own anything that wasn't purchased at the Salvation Army?" He started to push past Hudde.

Gordan may have been two inches shorter but was probably fifty pounds heavier, and he leaned into Kinkade and acted as if he nearly spilled one of the cups.

"Whoa, I almost got coffee all over your Armani! That was close! Come tell me about your adventures over some breakfast at the IHOP."

"Listen, Hudde. I hardly slept last night."

Gordan interrupted. "I know. I was just talking with the doorman."

Kinkade's head snapped in the direction of the door.

"Oh, don't be hard on the guy, Terrance!" He accentuated the name like they should be sipping tea with their pinkies up. "I guess he actually likes women, and they have some suspicions about you." Gordan showed some teeth in his fake smile. "I guess that confirms some of the rumors I've heard."

Kinkade balled his hands into fists and stepped into Hudde, ignoring the cups of coffee now.

"What the hell do you want?" he whispered.

"Oh, nothing special. I just wanted to make sure that Afghanistan trip with Crewbon went okay for you."

Kinkade leaned down to make eye contact with Hudde. "First, that trip was coded. I should have the agency start an investigation just for you bringing it up here. Second, you would be wise to remember who I work for and, maybe even more importantly, why they hired me."

Gordan grinned even wider and leaned forward, bumping Kinkade and pushing him back with his weight advantage. "What? You think you're dangerous now?" He continued pressing forward while balancing the two cups of coffee. "I'm sure they hired you because of your daddy, pretty much why everyone has your whole life."

Spittle flew from Kinkade's lips. "Fuck off," he hissed as he spun away and walked quickly toward the door, which the doorman now pulled open.

The doorman swallowed hard when Kinkade stared at him as he passed. Hudde followed and turned back, handing one of the cups to the uniformed man.

"Don't worry about him; I'm guessing he's moving soon."

The doorman looked Hudde up and down. "Mister, who are you anyway?"

"As far as he's concerned," Hudde nodded in the direction of the quickly walking away Kinkade, "I'm reality." Hudde spun himself and headed out into the dreary cold rain.

■ ■ ■

"This is unacceptable!" Director Smith had both hands flat on his desk, trying to show that he was at ease, but now he began tapping his right thumb to the beat of an unheard song.

"You know damned well that I can't produce an agent from four or five thousand miles away overnight." The chair in front of the Director's desk was inadequate for a man of John Stevens's girth, but he sat still and upright, locking his eyes on Smith's.

"This isn't some request to go over expense reports, Deputy Director. This is a directive from the President himself!" Now both thumbs were keeping time.

"Ben, my agent is looking into a Bolivian drug lord right now." He shrugged his shoulders very slightly. "I just don't understand what that would have to do with Dubois, or Crewbon, for that matter." Now he leaned forward.

Smith leaned back in his chair. "I never mentioned Crewbon."

Stevens pulled his chair closer and placed both his hands onto the desk; he could feel the warmth where Smith's hands had just been. "But this is about Crewbon. You just confirmed it."

"Nonsense. I didn't confirm anything." He stood and walked to the window.

"Regardless, I can't produce any reports that do not exist or make an agent appear who is so far away." Now Stevens had extracted himself from the small chair; he was intimidating in any room.

Smith turned back into the center of the room. "At least tell me the agent is moving in the correct direction. Maybe we can meet tomorrow. Maybe that would be acceptable under the circumstances."

"Under what circumstances?" Stevens's brows furrowed, and he placed both his hands on his hips. "Director, you need to fill me in so that I can help."

"You can help by getting your agent front and center ASAP. Whatever he is doing is of interest, and that's all I know. They seem upset. I can tell you that." Smith returned to his seat. "Get out of my office, and keep me informed."

Stevens didn't say anything. He just walked out of the office. He felt that he had learned quite a bit during this interaction. Maybe this is why a professional should be running this organization, instead of some political hack.

■ ■ ■

The Director of the CIA looked at the floor as he was being dressed down in front of Crewbon and director of the FBI, Matthew Slovianski, by the President.

"How the fuck can you not know where one of your agents is?" Dubois was pacing the floor, stopping momentarily in front of Smith, waiting for an answer.

"Director Slovianski, we're going to need a BOLO for this agent Hudde," Crewbon suggested.

"We can do that," Slovianski offered.

"That would be an 'Observe and report' only. We want to pick him up when and where when we are good and ready." Crewbon turned from the window he was looking out of. "Smith, you are to let us know when he returns to the States."

"Of course."

The door to the Oval Office opened. Everyone turned to look.

Kinkade entered. "Guess who I just had a conversation with!" He was obviously excited.

"Meeting adjourned. Everyone out." Crewbon began waving everyone to the door. "Not you." He pointed at Kinkade and shook his head. "No need for that BOLO or any actions by your people, Slovianski."

"Okay."

When only Kinkade, Crewbon, and the President were left in the room, Crewbon shut the door and returned to the window.

Crewbon was still shaking his head. He looked at Kinkade. "You never offer any information in a room full of people."

Kinkade furrowed his brows and shrugged his shoulders. "You were all hot on finding this guy and that was his boss and the guys who were going to look for him, right?"

Crewbon looked down at the floor and took a couple of deep breaths. Then he looked up at the President. "Sir, I would suggest you go back to working on Friday's speech to the United Nations. Terry and I can work this out in my office."

Dubois looked back and forth between the two men. "Yes. That seems like a good plan."

Crewbon placed his hand on the small of Kinkade's back and pushed him until they were out in the hall, heading to his office.

Neither spoke until the door closed behind them. Crewbon walked behind his desk, which had been built up under his directions so that he had to take two steps to get up and into his chair.

Kinkade never said so, but, to him, it looked ridiculously like some sort of miniature court room. He took his seat before the miniature judge.

Crewbon looked down at Kinkade. "Okay. Explain to me what happened."

Kinkade shrugged his shoulders. "He was waiting for me in the lobby this morning. Said he wanted to take me to breakfast."

"Did he say anything interesting?"

"Wanted to know how our Afghanistan trip went."

"*Our?* Did he ask about me by name?"

"Yeah. He mentioned you."

Crewbon closed his eyes and unconsciously began rubbing his left eyebrow as he practiced breathing slowly and deeply.

"I need you to find out what he knows or thinks he knows about any of our plans." Kinkade's eyebrows went up, a bit surprised. "I know, I know: 'Top Secret' and all that, but..." Crewbon paused, still thinking. Then he switched gears. "Terry, do you know why I selected you?"

"I expect that it had something to do with my father."

"No! Your father had nothing to do with your selection."

Kinkade's mouth turned up slightly.

"Your father most likely found out about your vaunted position whenever you told him about it. I read the reports and files about you and saw a man with many talents and a desire, a drive to go further, be more than a man living under the shadow of a powerful, domineering father."

Kinkade was nodding, happy with this assessment.

"Now this is a compliment. I saw a man not shackled with the…constraints… that many others place upon themselves. In you, I see a man destined for much greater things."

"Thank you, Mr. Crewbon. I appreciate that." He was pleased that someone saw him for who he felt he was.

"Now, tell me, Terry. Where does it stop for you? I know that you are successful and wealthy now — way beyond your family's wealth. Do you want more?"

Kinkade wanted to appear thoughtful, so he waited an appropriate time before responding, "I appreciate your confidence, sir. I desire only to stay with you after the President gets reelected. I can't say I've thought beyond that right now."

"I'm going to be very honest with you right now, Terry, I don't see you as a 'flag waver.' I think you care more about being on the winning team and getting the recognition that you deserve from all the hard work you've put in."

"Yes, sir. That's right."

"Please, Terry — in here, I'm just Victor." He didn't smile because he did own a mirror and knew how that looked. "I'm talking to my closest partner right now, not a hired hand. So tell me what it is that you want."

"Victor, you have described me better than anyone ever has. I'm flattered, to be honest. Yes, I want more. Yes, I want to be on the winning team. Whatever it takes."

"So look into the future and tell me what is going to happen out there in the world. What will America's role be?"

"Fuck, that's deep. If I had to say, I would have to take into account all of our travels. It seems nearly every country hates us or wants to take advantage of us. Our ability to conventionally control the world through strength is waning. I know, of course, we could nearly destroy the world with our nuclear arsenal, but with conventional weapons and forces — no. We can handle only one conflict at the moment without additional countries helping significantly."

Crewbon nodded. "Very good. Now give me more, with some additional details." He flipped his right hand over and waved at him as if he were saying, "Come along."

Kinkade nodded his head left to right as he thought. "Well, Dubois is going to allow Russia to return to their pre-Cold War borders. This will strengthen them greatly, and their influence will grow. If this Middle East peace deal is signed, Dubois has agreed to get the U.S. out of there altogether."

Crewbon was nodding, but he waved for more.

"Internally, the country could fold at any moment due to our financial obligations alone. We probably have the smallest Navy and Army since before WWII, and our Air Force is flying planes two times older than I am." He licked his lips and opened his eyes wide, deep in thought. "I'm willing to bet the Chinese will surpass our conventional forces in strength first, and soon."

Crewbon interrupted. "In twenty years, how old will you be?"

"Just fifty-seven. I hope that's not old."

"No, that's young in my book. But, with everything you described to me, how will you spend your retirement years?"

Kinkade chuckled. "I admitted that I hadn't thought about even two years from now!"

"So think about this. I will always need good men from different walks of life. What if I could carve out a kingdom for you to reign over, to control any way you see fit? I'm obviously talking about much more than a large plot of land — I mean much more."

Kinkade squinted. "What do you mean?"

"What if I could give you France or Sweden, I don't know. I'll let you choose."

Kinkade sat back in the chair and let out a loud breath.

"Terry, think about all the things you have said here. Then add in a large Islamic Caliphate with all the resources that they will be able to muster working with Russia, controlling almost all of Africa and most of Western Europe. They will pressure China to call in the debt that America owes them. You know what would happen then."

"America would go bankrupt. There would be anarchy." His eyes went blank as he stared at the side of the desk.

"America is bankrupt financially and morally, Terry. You have been there every step of the way. In fact, you have been instrumental, I would say. Why not reach for more and see this to the end?"

"The country?" Terry asked.

"In the future, there will be three superpowers, but America will not be one of them." He paused to see what kind of reaction Kinkade had to this news. There was none. "You can keep your head in the sand and hope that the inevitable doesn't happen — or you can pledge loyalty to me and rise as I do."

"What about Dubois? Where does he stand with all this?"

Crewbon sighed. "He believes that, after the coming strife, which — I assure you — he has been working to bring about long before he ran for office, he will set up the perfect socialist empire. He dreams of being a benevolent dictator for life." He allowed his lips to curl up so that it looked almost like he was smiling. "I think he will be very disappointed when he realizes what actually will transpire. Your star does not have to be hitched to his wagon. What do you say, Terry? Are you with me?"

He'd made his best pitch, and he knew that it was time to wait for an answer.

Kinkade's mind was racing. "I guess I knew all along that all this would end badly. I'm with you, Victor. Whatever it takes, I think I would like that kingdom."

"Very good. First thing you need to do is make contact with this Hudde agent and find out what he knows and who else may know anything. You have my complete authority to negotiate any price to get silence. Nothing else will suffice."

"And if there is no price?"

Crewbon walked down and around his desk, grabbing Terry by the elbow and leading him toward the door. "You've never failed me on any task I've given you. I trust your judgement. Understand that this plan is at the precipice of being on auto-pilot. That's when some people relax and allow something small to foil well-thought-out plans. You and I will not be one of those people."

They arrived at the door. "Keep your mind on the task at hand. Then you and I will usher in a New World Order. You can't possibly know, but there are hundreds of millions of supporters out there just waiting to be led, waiting for a sign. So much depends on me…" he squeezed Terry's elbow even harder "…and you."

"You can depend on me, Victor. I will not let you down."

"Call me when you make contact with your fellow agent."

14

Gordan Hudde looked down at his phone to read the text that had just come through: "u r alone" was all it said, and, although Gordan did not recognize the number, he was sure it was from Deputy Director Stevens.

What the fuck do I do now? Gordan thought. He needed to get to Kinkade, he knew that much. But he just didn't know enough about the entire situation to take any drastic measures...yet.

He dropped the rental keys into the box available for returns. He was heading into airport parking to pick up his truck when his phone began to vibrate.

"Yeah." Hudde didn't recognize this number, either.

"Kinkade here, Gordan."

Gordan said nothing. He just walked and listened.

"You still there?"

"What can I do for you, Terrance?"

"Look, Gordan. There's no need for us to be at odds with each other. We play for the same team, after all."

"Alright, I'll bite. What do you want?"

Kinkade chuckled. "It's not like that. I have an offer for you, and I think you should hear me out, give me a chance."

Gordan was silent for a few steps.

"You going somewhere?" Kinkade asked, hearing the jets in the background.

"Not just yet, Terry. Why don't you tell me what you can offer."

Hudde could hear him breathing. "No, Gordan. This is face-to-face kind of business. Why don't we meet?"

"You could have done that over breakfast earlier."

"It hadn't presented itself yet. Don't be scared." He paused, and Gordan thought he could hear him grin. "It will be a generous offer, trust me."

"So Dubois or Crewbon just gave you some new instructions?"

Kinkade tried to chuckle again. "You're a funny guy. I've got to hand it to you."

"Okay, then. Name a public place."

"Oh, Gordan. You're scared of me. That's too bad. I promise that this is legitimate. How about that mall near Columbia, in the food court, about 13:30 hours, and, of course, you come alone."

"Right." Gordan hung up. Just being on the phone with Kinkade made him feel slimy. He headed straight back to his townhome for a shower, a meal, and some decent sleep, he hoped.

■ ■ ■

Victor Crewbon hung up from Kinkade and immediately redialed.

Bob picked up the phone from the nightstand on the small coffee table. There was enough daylight so that, now, the neon sign outside the cheap motel just north of Washington, DC no longer dominated the light inside the dirty room.

"Yes."

Crewbon spoke in his native language. "Two men will meet at 1:30 tomorrow afternoon. One will, I'm sure, be dressed very well in a suit and tie, and that man is with us. The other is our enemy. He must be taken care of permanently and quietly."

"Understood."

"When you have completed this task, know that, within days, even hours, the sign for all our brothers will be given, and your plans…" he paused, searching for the correct words, "…*assignments* will begin in earnest. Just remain silent, and be in place to begin."

"Allah's will be done," Bob said before he returned the phone to the table top. He turned to his two remaining men.

"We have one more task before the real war begins."

■ ■ ■

Nearly a block away from his townhome, Gordan pulled his truck over to the side of the road and hit the garage-door remote.

He watched for an explosion from a relatively safe distance and then waited five more minutes before moving forward and stopping in his driveway.

"You're a paranoid motherfucker," he said to himself, and yet he could not stop himself from leaving the truck outside and heading in on foot, looking for anything out of order. There was nothing, so he pulled the truck in and closed the door behind him.

Now he went through his checklist for booby traps and bugs that he conducted every time he returned after any trip. He first opened his main electrical panel, where a small blue light indicated that no one had shut off the main power. Gordan checked for pressure mats under the carpets, motion detectors, and trip wires.

Gordan locked up and then went to his final place to look for a trap—the refrigerator. Once he was satisfied that it was okay to do so, he removed a cold beer and took it into the shower, where he stood under scalding hot water while he sipped the ice-cold brew.

Gordan wanted to call Deputy Director Stevens, but he knew that all the evidence he had was circumstantial and each item alone meant nothing. Gordan was not one to cry "wolf," and he could guess that Stevens would not be comfortable trying to enlist help from anyone outside the agency.

Officially, no one would react to the info Gordan had at his disposal right now, especially when you considered who he was trying to implicate. Gordan's one "ace in the hole" would have been Foster with his firsthand knowledge, but now he had been killed. Of course, Hudde suspected that Kinkade, Crewbon, or maybe even Dubois had had a hand in this, and he knew if he said that out loud anywhere right now, they would lock him up and toss the key.

Kinkade's meeting had to be a trap. If what Hudde suspected was true, they had to remove him from the equation as well.

Hudde's brain screamed, *"For what?"* and he knew that was his weakest position. Just what were they up to? He wished he had some backup for this meeting tomorrow, and he called Little Creek, looking to see if he could find some of Foster's teammates. He was put on hold, and he hung up before he could see if anyone would tell him if they were still here after the funeral.

He lay back onto his sofa and tried to maintain focus, but the sunlight was fading, and so was consciousness.

He woke up just before dawn the following morning. Refreshed from sleep, he made some coffee and downed a microwaved egg sandwich before showering.

Everyone shows up an hour to an hour and a half early for meetings. Gordan went to his walk-in closet and began to dress. He had never operated on American soil before, but his style of dressing overseas was more than acceptable to him here as well. Blue jeans and a dark t-shirt first. He reached for his shoulder rig and slid open the slide to his .45. He dropped a single round into the chamber, allowed the slide back, and then slowly dropped the hammer. Then he slid home a full magazine before placing two more full magazines into the double pocket on the leather rig under his left arm. The .45 slid easily under his right arm.

Gordan reached for the simple-looking canvas belt and slipped it through the loops around his waist. Five feet of piano wire had been woven into the fabric, and a small, sturdy knife was hidden in the heavy belt buckle. Its T-shaped handle could be grasped and pulled quickly, leaving about two deadly inches of blade sticking out between the index and middle fingers. He smiled, knowing that this was not much more than a party trick, but he never went anywhere without it.

Gordan rolled up his right pant leg and slid on the ankle holster that would hold a stainless .38 snubby. Gordan hated shooting it because the grip was too small for his oversized hand, but, in an emergency, he would be grateful that it was there.

He slid on a dark blue hoodie and covered that with a 4XL denim jacket. He was able to load the deep pockets with a speed loader for the snubbie and an ambidextrous three-and-a-half-inch flip blade while still leaving room. He bounced on his toes, and nothing made any noise. The load had to be at least 100 pounds less than he usually carried overseas, so he felt light on his feet.

Always the Boy Scout, he grabbed a small duffle bag and threw in several bottles of water and a few meal-replacement bars before heading for his truck. It was always best to be prepared not to come back for a few days.

Hudde found the mall just after 0900 hrs. He circled the entire structure on the access road, dodging what was probably late-arriving employees who knew exactly where they were going, cutting across the parking lots at dangerous speeds. He noted the parking garage and the quickest ways to get back to the streets.

The mall was shaped like a boomerang, one end anchored by a Sears with the signs for the food court nearby. Then the structure slowly warped off to the northwest. On that end, there was a huge freestanding movie theater complex and then what appeared to Gordan to be a largely unorganized group of chain eateries that he guessed would make driving and parking on a busy night dangerous. This is where he parked.

He looked up as he walked past the theater and noticed that the latest superhero movie was playing. He looked at his watch and thought *what the hell.* Shrugging his shoulders, he headed inside. He'd always had to wait for the Blu-Ray releases when he was working, so this was a treat. He got a ticket and squeezed into a seat all the way in the back.

■ ■ ■

Crewbon's remaining team of Bob, Dan, and Eddy arrived in the white van about 45 minutes early. They saw the same food-court signs, and Bob pulled over to allow Dan and Eddy to head inside to get into position. Bob then pulled out to the far reaches of that parking lot, where he might see the target park and enter.

Dan went straight to a counter and purchased a pretzel and an iced tea, taking up a seat where anyone coming into the food court from the one outside door would have to walk right past him. Anyone entering from the mall would walk straight toward him regardless if they came from the Sears or the mall.

Eddy found the escalator and took up a position above the food court, giving him the ability to scan not only a large area for the target but also some of the handsome young men that appeared to be working in many of the stores.

■ ■ ■

Hudde exited the fire door near the screen of the theater. He squinted, even though the sun was covered by clouds. He was looking at the large anchor store on the north end of the mall. He had enjoyed the creativity of the fiction he'd just watched, still enamored by characters he had grown up reading about. But now was the time to ramp up his senses and be prepared for the worst. He doubted Kinkade would start something inside, but he couldn't rule it out.

Hudde grabbed his beard and pulled down through it before setting his chin and heading inside. He found the escalator and headed up, and then he walked slowly toward the food court he knew was on the other end. He attempted to be casual, keeping an eye out for a tail or for anyone who appeared to be out of place. What made it easier was that it was a weekday and the traffic was fairly light and made up mostly of women shoppers and employees from the stores themselves.

Hudde picked up a possible Tango the moment the smells of the food below came to his nose. The man looked to be from the Middle East or the Mediterranean area, for sure, with his dark skin and hair, a heavy brow and nose. Gordan stopped just inside and watched as the man scanned the area, trying to look without appearing to be interested. Yeah — this was someone of interest.

Gordan ignored him and headed down the escalator, using this moment to scan the area below. There were some teenage boys talking too loudly and pushing each other around, a businessman in a cheap suit, some girls in some kind of business attire he did not recognize, and one man who could have been the bookend to the guy upstairs. Hudde felt sure the two were together.

Ignoring both men, Gordan got himself a coffee from a pastry shop and found a seat from which he could see both men, using his peripheral vision. He tried to look relaxed and sipped his coffee, admiring the legs of a businesswoman in a tight skirt. She noticed and smiled but then sat with her back to Gordan. A young guy in a white shirt and tie arrived shortly and took a seat across from her.

Gordan saw Kinkade walking briskly from the large opening of the Sears store. He stopped briefly, made eye contact with Hudde, and made a beeline toward him.

"Gordan." Kinkade acknowledged him and then looked down at the bright plastic chair.

Gordan pushed the chair out with his foot. He bet himself that Kinkade would wipe the chair first with a napkin; he lost when he merely tipped the chair up to lose any crumbs, and then he took a seat.

Kinkade eyed him up and down. "We agreed to come unarmed."

"I'm guessing you're packing, too," Gordan noted. "I'm willing to bet you don't want a shootout in a suburban mall. It wouldn't look good on the news."

Kinkade smiled a fake smile. He looked around the food court but never allowed his eyes to settle on anyone or anything. If he was working with those two men, Gordan thought he was doing a great job of ignoring them.

"Hey, Terrance. It's your dime." He turned both his hands palms up and shrugged his shoulders while raising his eyebrows.

Kinkade turned his head and focused. "You first have to acknowledge that we are all on the same team." He looked at Hudde expectantly.

Hudde just stared back.

"We believe you may be digging into something that could put some very important plans in jeopardy."

Gordan pointed at him. "When you say 'we,' just who are you talking about?"

Kinkade rolled his eyes. "Everyone knows I'm working directly for the President."

"That's funny." Hudde rubbed his chin. "I thought you were chummy with Crewbon."

Kinkade closed his eyes and took a deep breath. "Come on. I'm trying to be sincere here. Yes, Victor Crewbon is the President's Chief of Staff, so I work closely with him."

Hudde pointed again but this time did some small circles with his finger. "So the three of you came up with a plan to meet with… what was he at the time…the Number Two Most Wanted on the terrorist list?"

Kinkade smiled. "Oh, your Boy Scout sensibilities are hurt? Get over yourself, Gordan. The enemy of my enemy is my friend. I'm sure you've heard that before." Kinkade shook his head. "I know I don't have to tell you how we do deals sometimes. You can't be such a baby after everything you've been through."

Hudde spoke through gritted teeth. "I'd love to just hug this out, but I know of only three people who know about that meeting: You, Crewbon, and a Navy SEAL who just got himself killed down in Texas." His eyes narrowed while he stared at the man across from him.

Kinkade's eyes got wide, and he shrugged his shoulders. "Nothing I know about…I swear."

Gordan nodded slowly. "I almost believe you, but then why are your boys pulling the short hairs of the Deputy Director? I didn't tell him anything."

Kinkade scratched his nose. "Now who's lying? Why is Stevens trying to cover for you if he doesn't know what you're up to?" He looked down at the table and shook his head before looking back up to make eye contact with Hudde. "Stevens never could see my potential. I think he's incompetent."

"Yeah, well. Aren't you the expert at that?" Hudde smirked.

Kinkade took another deep breath.

"I've been authorized to make you a deal, not to start a fight."

"If you guys are working on behalf of the country, why do you need to offer me anything? Why did you need to kill a hero or destroy a man's career?"

Kinkade closed his eyes and rubbed his temples with a thumb and forefinger before speaking.

"Look, I don't know anything about a SEAL, okay? I also only know that Stevens gave the president the run-around when they asked about you. He chose to fuck with the wrong guys. Why don't we talk about what's best for Gordan Hudde?"

Gordan sat up and placed both his elbows on the table. "Here's what I think, Terrance. I think there is no holy trinity between the President, Crewbon, and you. I think they needed some muscle that could be bought off because you're so eager to be out of daddy's shadow."

Kinkade started to interrupt.

"No, wait. There's more. I think you don't have a clue as to what's really going on. You see, I just got back from a trip to Turkey, and guess what? Victor Crewbon isn't a Crewbon after all. Yeah, that's right. He was a little orphan bastard *jihadi* in training over there when he was unofficially adopted by Andrei and his barren American wife."

Kinkade was paying attention now.

"Yeah. Seems that daddy Andrei was born with a silver spoon in his mouth, and life was so easy that he felt bad and wanted to spread the wealth through socialism. Of course, he never gave up his father's billions. And while I'm at it, I'd like to point out that it seems to me that everything your boy Dubois has been doing since getting himself elected has been weakening us here and abroad."

Kinkade sat back, allowing his lungs to empty as he did. He was offended but only because Hudde had started his rant by doubting Kinkade's important part in this scheme, his place in the inner sanctum.

Kinkade began nodding before speaking. "Yes. Okay, I have heard of plans for after America. After everything you've seen out there, you don't sometimes do the same?" He made his lips pout and shook his head. "I just can't believe the great Gordan Hudde doesn't have a "bug out" plan."

Hudde was unsure of where this was going, so he played along. "Alright. I see the possibilities out there, but what are you suggesting? What should I be doing?" He offered Kinkade the chance to be smarter and keep him talking at the same time.

Kinkade visibly relaxed. He turned his right palm up. "You know I can't tell you everything that I know."

Hudde nodded, following every word. "You have to offer something."

"What I can tell you is that America is never going to be the same. Some of the people who have sent you into harm's way are not looking out for your best interests, Gordan. In twenty years, you will not be able to recognize this country."

Gordan kept playing, shrugging his heavy shoulders. "I don't get it. What can I do to stop it from happening?"

"That's just it. You can't." He chuckled. "One man can't change a course that's already been set. It's time that you look out for yourself." He pointed at him to accentuate the point.

Gordan put both hands on his head and sat back, taking in and letting out a deep breath. The two men were still in place… watching.

"So I should just run off and hide?"

Feeling like a hook was nearly set, Kinkade leaned in and placed his elbows on the table. "I always felt you were a bit of a flag waver, but I can tell you that a man like you could go off very wealthy, no need to hide," he finished, with a hint of a smile out of one side of his mouth.

Gordan stared a hole right through him. "Maybe I just like killing people."

Kinkade stared back for a moment and then laughed out loud. "Yeah, I buy that. But I have to say, you've been doing it for peanuts." He raised an eyebrow. "Why not, Gordan? Why not reach just a bit further and grasp the golden ring I'm offering? You can ride off to whatever it is you want to do."

Gordan put his hands together in front of his face. "What kind of peanuts do your guys offer?"

Kinkade slapped the table with the palm of his hand, reeling in his fish. "There you go! That's a man I can work with!" He nodded and smiled.

Hudde smiled back. "I want whatever deal you got."

Kinkade made a big deal of frowning. "Now, don't get greedy. Remember, I came in on the ground floor. You're just talking 'go away' money. My package is a whole other level, brother."

"I'll bite. Then what does my plan get me?"

Kinkade was beyond happy. This was going to work, and he was finishing off his plan in his mind on just how he would benefit the most as they spoke.

"You're a bit younger than me, Hudde. What do you think it would take to live comfortably for the rest of your life?"

"Fuck, you know how to put a guy on the spot." He paused. "Two or three million, maybe?"

"Jesus, Hudde, you sell yourself short. I'd say at least five million. Everyone underestimates how much retirement will take. Don't find yourself looking for work at an advanced age."

You grew up with a silver spoon in your mouth while I busted my ass, Gordan thought.

"Let me see if I got this straight. I take five million in cash, drop any questions I have, and turn my back on America?"

"America doesn't care about you. Why do you care back? Anyway, that's exactly how it would work, no other strings attached." Kinkade raised both eyebrows, waiting.

"The thing is, Kinkade, I don't trust you. I don't trust the people you work for."

Kinkade nodded. "I don't blame you, I guess. Tell you what. I'll set up a new laptop with nothing but your new Swiss account with lots of zeros on it. We can meet up later and then…" he smiled and nodded. "…Nothing. You just head off into the sunset a happy and very wealthy man."

Hudde rubbed his beard. "You know what, Terry? Fuck this place, fuck my bosses, and fuck your buddies. You show up with that and a briefcase with $100,000 in cash — you know, for immediate spending money — and I'll believe you." Gordan opened his eyes wide and held out his right hand.

Kinkade studied his face, started to grin, and then he nodded. "That works for me." He took Hudde's hand firmly. "Welcome to easy street, son." Kinkade stood and made sure his tie was perfect. "I'll be in touch soon."

Kinkade turned and walked out. Gordan did not notice any eye contact made between Kindade and the other two; no communication either between the two men still here, watching. Kinkade headed straight out through the big chain anchor store, never looking back.

Hudde picked up his cup and went in the same direction, stopping at a trash container and then turning quickly and heading back into the heart of the mall. Both men had already moved from their earlier positions to follow but then had to stop and wait, confirming to Hudde that they were with Kinkade.

He headed straight to the opposite end of the mall, walking quickly at first, slowing as he neared the big store where he had entered. He stepped into a smaller store and used the displays to see that both men were still with him.

Hudde saw a bookstore across from his current spot and walked into it slowly, taking in the magazines closer to the cashier. Then he drifted toward the deep back wall. The man upstairs had to walk all the way around to the opposite walkway to keep an eye on Hudde, but he was still unable to see him in the back of the store.

The ground-floor man paced outside the store and occasionally stole a glance inside to confirm Hudde hadn't snuck out a back entrance.

Hudde drifted back to the wood magazine rack near the registers, where he was now visible to both men. These were not men from the agency — they were just too amateurish to be seasoned agents. He picked up a magazine about military weapons and ran his hand through his beard.

Where was Kinkade recruiting from?

Hudde went to the cashier, paid for the magazine, and started into the mall at a quicker pace than before only to drop down into an uncomfortable plastic chair and begin to read.

The other man found his own uncomfortable plastic chair, where he sat nearly within conversational proximity. Hudde looked up and around and then returned to his reading; the man upstairs was on his phone. Hudde was sure that these two were becoming anxious with his lack of activity.

He had to consider that this meeting was just an opportunity to get him out on the surface so that they could eliminate him from their list of problems — and that the two men following him were his executioners.

■ ■ ■

It was warm enough that Bob rolled the driver's-side window down and parked along the curb at the center of the mall. He parked far enough from the entrances that he did not impede the flow of traffic picking up or dropping off people nearby. However, the third time the security-marked Cushman drove past much slower, and the woman inside strained her neck to look inside the van as she slipped past.

The Cushman then changed its pattern from the previous two trips past and turned up inside the parking lot. Bob watched as it turned back and appeared to be doubling back to go past him once again. He put the van in gear and drove out to find a spot where he could park and wait. He couldn't afford to have "If you see something, say something" ruin their efforts.

Eddy grew impatient looking down from the second level of the decadent mall. He turned his back and leaned against the railing, trying to look calm. He took out the phone that Bob had given him from the box of phones that they would use as triggering devices once this mission was accomplished.

Once Bob picked up, Eddy whispered, "Why do we waste all this time? Let me kill him now, and then we can start with our real task."

"Patience, my brother," Bob said. "We have not yet seen the sign to even begin our mission. Do not worry. Our time is coming. Besides, we must ask questions of this one."

Eddy growled, "Even the mannequins offend me here." He looked into the store to his front and shook his head. "It would do my heart good to watch these infidels run from my blade."

"Do not let your personal feelings get in the way of the work before us. We will make the entire country tremble with fear, much the same as that glorious day in September."

"I thirst for that day."

■ ■ ■

Gordan allowed his eyes to scan both of the men following him. The one closest to him had put his head in his hands, as if he were sleeping, while the man above had his back against the railing and appeared to be on a phone.

The casual mall noises allowed Gordan to get up and leave the magazine. He headed into the anchor store at the end of the mall, well before the man who had been seated near him looked up and noticed. That man then needed to whistle to get his partner to turn back and see that their target was on the move.

Gordan turned the corner, where he lost contact with his pursuers. Then he sprinted towards the exit. He hit the doors and then ran in the direction of the movie theater and his truck. He did not stop running until he was breathing a bit heavy in the driver's seat. Pulling out his phone, he dialed the Deputy Director's office. If they could manage a team to pick these men up without alerting Kinkade or Crewbon, that would be very beneficial.

His call was picked up by the CIA operator. They could not put the call through, and how else could he be helped? *Fuck!*

One pull on his beard and he made a decision. He turned the wheel and headed back to the mall anchor store.

He quickly saw the upstairs suspect now scanning the parking lot from the sidewalk outside. Gordan turned his truck and drove past the individual who momentarily could not help but show his amazement and good fortune. He pulled out his phone and called for his ride.

Gordan saw him picked up by a white van and he politely allowed some traffic to go before him so that the van could catch up at a safe distance before he pulled out into street traffic.

15

Crewbon paced the Oval Office while he spoke on the phone with Kinkade.

"No, Terry, that is brilliant! I expected nothing else, to be honest. We would have been satisfied even if it were three or four times that amount! Now, Terry, if the plans somehow fall through, or if agent Hudde fails to meet you later, you just make sure that you are at Andrews at 0200 on Saturday morning. Understand?"

Dubois looked up from his United Nations speech that would be delivered Friday afternoon. "Issues?"

Crewbon shook his head. "Okay, then, agent Kinkade, we will see you then."

Crewbon walked behind the President to look out the window. "No issues at all. In fact, I feel a bit uneasy because of the way everything seems to be working out perfectly."

He found himself staring at the place on Dubois's neck where his knife would first pierce the flesh. He was beginning to feel a bit euphoric, as his lifelong ambitions, his plans, where about to come true.

"Hey, Lemme, what do you say we relive some of the old days, and Saturday, we sneak out of here with the smallest staff? What do you say? Leave most of the press, take the smallest Secret Service team, and head out —a bit like the old campaign days?"

The president swiveled in his seat to make eye contact. "My wife…"

Crewbon interrupted. "Oh, Lemme — especially the wife." He tried his best smile. "We can have some brandy and smoke some cigars on the way to Israel. Besides if I hear one more thing about her 'agenda,' I may toss her from the plane myself."

Dubois shook his head. "Victor, that's …well…awful funny!" he chuckled. "Sure. Let's talk about it. In fact, whatever you think is alright. Just make it so."

■ ■ ■

Damn it!

Kinkade was now a bit angry with himself that he hadn't offered Hudde a larger sum of money. He could have really added to his own nest egg; probably too late to change it now.

He looked at the computer screen and made the necessary keystrokes to create the $5 million account in the Swiss bank. He ran his hand over the cash, packed tightly in the small leather briefcase just off to his right. It was too bad that he couldn't devise a way to save it, but if his plan worked, he was going to be $5 million richer. Why be worried about a measly $100K? He duplicated the account onto a brand-new iPad that he could leave for Hudde to find.

It was very satisfying to be so close to the top of command, never worrying about the rules that were set up for the unwashed. He smiled and looked up, imagining what his father would think of this.

He took a moment to pour a glass of wine before using the laptop to search for just the right piece of real estate that he could use for the next part of his plan.

16

Gordan knew how difficult it was to follow someone in traffic, even with additional units. This van was trying to follow Gordan in rush-hour traffic alone. He pulled into a diner. He could eat and continue to try to make contact with Stevens to get some backup, if needed. It would also make the guys behind him have to wait some more.

Gordan gave up on the CIA headquarters building and used an emergency number that Stevens had once offered.

When Stevens picked up, he just said, "Go."

"Roger that. I've picked up a tail, and I was hoping we had some local assets. Maybe we could pull a switch on them."

"I found my office closed and locked this afternoon with my personal belongings boxed and ready to go."

"Shit…you're fired?" Gordan was disappointed, not surprised.

"No, not yet. I'd say I've been 'sequestered.'"

Gordan leaned forward to look at the white van as it tried to park in a position where the occupants could see into the window.

"Hey, boss. What are the odds? The van that's been following me all day is from Texas."

"The men responsible for the Fosters massacre?"

"It's gotta be." Gordan and Stevens did not speak for a moment. "Hey, boss. You think you might be able to get a call into Little Creek and see if some of Foster's friends might be up for a bit of payback?"

Stevens made a small, growling noise. "Aren't they deployed?"

Gordan shook his head. "Back for the funeral, I would imagine."

"I'll reach out. What should I tell them?"

"Give them my old call sign, if you can find Foster's old Captain — um… Hernandez, if I remember correctly. Tell them that "Reaper" needs some help and that it's darker than anything they ever have done before."

"I can do that. This is the first and last time I'll ever use this phone. Can you tell me anything else?"

"Only that it's bad — real bad. The hair on the back of my neck tells me."

"Be careful."

"Roger that."

Gordan took his time. He got an extra cup of coffee before ordering dinner. He guessed that there was an argument going on in the van along the lines of whether to send someone in for food or have them come in separately to use the bathroom.

It was getting dark, and he had been there for hours.

The driver finally slid out from the left side of the van, stretched, and walked into the front of the diner.

Gordan could almost hear the man as he began ordering some takeout.

Gordan waited until they handed a cardboard tray with three cups of coffee or tea on it for the driver, standing at the register. Then he left forty bucks and headed toward the exit. He waved at the waitress, knowing that she would be happy with the tip, and smiled at the Middle Eastern-looking fellow, who looked back into the kitchen and then back out to his van before he hung his head and followed. He knew that he could not even wait for their own chow.

Gordan heard the waitress say, "But what about the rest of your order?" But he did not turn to look back. He smiled, knowing the team following him would have only extra caffeine in their stomachs and fluid in their bladders.

Gordan slid into his truck and started out, looking for the type of location that he would need to put his own plan into action. He needed to turn the tables. He didn't want to do it anywhere near the public, and he couldn't wait to hear back from Stevens.

■ ■ ■

Stevens had another throwaway phone to his ear. "That's right, Captain. Reaper believes he has eyes on the Foster-family killers."

There was a long silence. "Anytime, anywhere."

"That's good. I'll let him know. Stand by."

■ ■ ■

Hudde pulled out into traffic. He didn't hurry, and he didn't take corners or switch lanes without a turn signal. He didn't want to lose his "friends."

Now it was well after dark. He went to a business park that he had driven by earlier. He hoped he could find an empty business where he could confront the three men behind him and find out what information they had to offer. He didn't want to fire a weapon because he didn't have a silencer, and he didn't feel like being up all night trying to clean a crime scene. That wasn't his specialty, anyway.

He pondered whether he could drive these men out to the country but wasn't satisfied that he could successfully set up an ambush without knowing the landscape in advance.

No. Getting them somehow into close quarters, his own specialty, so that they, too, would find it impossible to fire a shot would allow him to gain the upper hand.

Gordan cruised the parking lots, looking for a business that appeared suitable. All the buildings looked the same: Two stories high, some with large bay roll-up doors for bringing in vehicles. Some were chest-high for bringing in stock or product.

There were many locations without identifying markings. There was a company that installed electronics in cars, an insurance agent's office, and there was a shop dedicated to upgrading the off-road capabilities of trucks. Nobody appeared to be burning the midnight oil in any of the businesses.

The parking lots consisted of a lazy "S" pattern, and the white van would appear behind Gordan at just the moment that Gordan would round the next bend.

As Gordan rounded the last bend, he noticed that the business in the last location had a cheap-looking sign with the address and "parts" in larger letters. He parked next to a panel truck that was directly under a "dusk to dawn" light that hung twenty-five feet off the ground and directed its light nearly straight down on top of the unoccupied truck.

Gordan was at the door before his tail had pulled around the building at the far end of the parking lot. Gordan readied his lock-picking tools in his hand as he approached but was surprised to find the steel door a bit ajar. He had to really put his back into opening the door and understood why the door was not fully closed.

Inside there was a short plywood entryway offering a second, cheap wooden door at the opposite end. On the door, a sheet of paper hung, taped at eye level: "Please see Kevin" was written in red ink in three-inch high letters. Gordan bit down on a small flashlight and picked the door in seconds.

Inside, it was like a cave. Gordan closed his eyes to allow them to adjust as much as they could. When he opened them, he could see the shapes of ten-foot-high metal shelving extending from where he stood further back into the facility, where the metal disappeared like the bones of a beast entering deeper water. Gordan walked further toward the back of the building, passing several more rows of the shelves. As he stepped past the last shelf, he observed a small office built from the same plywood as the entrance farther along the back wall. It had dim light coming from an office-door window.

■ ■ ■

Bob was losing patience with his men. After all they had accomplished — training and fighting in Afghanistan, sneaking into America from Mexico, finding and keeping work for nearly three years, finding and killing the Navy SEAL and his family, and now finding the CIA agent that his *Khalīfah* had designated as needing to meet his death — all this was ignored because his remaining men were tired, hungry, and needed to take a piss.

"Silence!" He turned and sneered at Eddy, who mumbled under his breath but lowered his eyes.

Bob turned back to look at the dark, open parking lot as he almost reached the last building. They would creep along at walking speed so they would not alert the CIA agent in the blue pickup truck further ahead of them.

"We must be getting close to something important for this man. Why else would he take such an indirect route?"

He suddenly slammed the van to a halt.

"What is it?" whispered Dan from the passenger seat, and he leaned forward toward the windscreen.

"He has stopped. I believe I saw the last door close just now."

Eddy made a grunting noise, and Bob did not turn to look at him. "By all means, get out and relieve yourself."

Eddy jumped out the back, and the men at the front could hear the heavy stream against the pavement behind them.

Dan whispered, although there was no need to. "What do you think he is doing?"

Bob looked at Dan now. "I have heard about secret drop houses where the CIA often keeps and maintains weapons and surveillance equipment. Maybe they do this in America as well."

Dan nodded slowly. "If we were to kill him here, we could raid their own arsenal to use it against them later."

Bob threw it into park and turned off the engine. "We do this here and now."

■ ■ ■

Gordan reached into one of the small boxes on the shelf in front of him. His gloved fingers came out with a few washers, and, in the next box, they were slightly larger.

Gordan peeked into the window of the small plywood office. It held several five-foot-tall metal file cabinets against the back wall. The light he had seen was from a small goose-necked desk lamp on a desk. A desktop computer was also on the desk, with cables running to the back wall for power, Internet access, and a printer that was on the floor next to an oscillating fan.

A clock radio was also plugged into the wall, and the blinking time showed either that the building had lost power or that the unit was used only as a radio.

Gordan stood behind the desk and closed his eyes. He ran his hand down his Spartan-like beard.

He opened his eyes. Anyone paying attention would say that they looked greener than just moments ago.

Opening the drawers, Gordan found some tape. He taped several pieces of paper across the only window, leaving the bottom of the paper unsecured. Then he positioned the fan and pulled up on the button so that, once it was on, it oscillated from one front corner to the other, making the paper across the window dance on each pass. He turned the small button on the top of the lamp to find that there were three light settings. He turned it to its brightest and bent the gooseneck so that the lamp was directed toward the door.

Gordan turned around and flicked on the radio. It was on low, but he found the country-western music agreeable. He turned it up before leaving the office, closing the door behind him. The second row of shelving had what he needed next—a rolling ladder so that people could access the upper shelves easily. He stepped on the wheel release so that the ladder rolled easily to the plywood walkway built into the first six feet of the small shop. He pushed it against the wall, dropped the ladder back onto its feet, and climbed to the top of the ladder. He stepped carefully onto the structure to ensure it held his weight comfortably. At the edge, now four feet above the interior door, Gordan could reach up and grasp the overhead steel beam that ran overhead. He stood there in the dark, waiting to see if the bait had been taken.

The papers waved in the office window below and made it appear as if there was movement inside the office. Gordan smiled.

17

Terry Kinkade stood in the darkness of the front lawn and smiled. This location would work perfectly for his plan. The first location he had scouted, closer to Washington, DC, was too pedestrian. This location was close to Andrews Airbase in case this dragged out closer to early Saturday morning, but it was surrounded on all sides by a wood line. The driveway sloped down to the street, probably a hundred yards or more. Then, once at the house, it swooped down and around to the basement level, ten feet lower than the front of the house. A garage or small barn was back there with a basketball backboard and rim set up.

Kinkade looked up the few steps to the front porch. The house was in great need of new paint, as it had stood empty for many years. Only the front door had been painted in the last decade, and it was a ghastly color. The wood was warping badly and as he tiptoed up the stairs, he reflected on how glad he was he hadn't put on any extra weight.

The highway actually ran behind the house, but the road noise was minimal, due to the heavy trees, brush, and the creek that flowed around the back of the home and then ran under the on/ off ramp. Henson Creek continued to run southeast. Kinkade shrugged his shoulders. It didn't matter where it went, and the steady sound of rushing waters would help conceal any noise.

He turned and looked south from the front porch. He couldn't see any other home. Almost directly across the street, following the same route as the creek, was a fittingly named service road called "Woodland." At the corner was a warehouse-style carpet business, and he made a mental note not to schedule anything during working hours so that it would lessen the chance anyone there would stumble upon his activities.

He slid back into what he considered to be his "junker" — a nearly two-year-old Cadillac Escalade — and followed the driveway down and around the back of the house. He opened the back tailgate and pulled out a large, black nylon duffle bag. He carried it up the wooden stairs to the back door, where he picked the lock and entered the kitchen of the old colonial.

In the front room, there were heavy drapes covering the windows. Kinkade made sure they were all closed and then turned on a battery-powered lantern. He slid the bag over to the front door and unzipped it. He began to pull out dark-green items and place them onto the floor in front of him. When he was done, he had twenty pounds of C-4 explosives and several different triggering devices before him. He first peeled the adhesive tape off the individual bars of the C-4 and placed them firmly onto the door around the frame, working in. He had enough to nearly cover the door. He took out the roll of "detonation cord" and tied a "det knot" every eighteen inches. He pushed a knot into each block of explosives so that the detonation cord was now connecting each block of explosives.

Next he punctured one of the bricks of explosives at the top of the door on its exposed side, one above the door's handle, and then one at the floor. He placed wood screws into the door jamb opposite the punctured explosives. He used simple battery-powered pull switches to arm the detonation caps above the door and at handle level. A small nine-volt battery fit into the unit.

On the floor, he attached a pull switch that used a time fuse attached to a blasting cap that was simply taped to a long piece of detonation cord. He rolled this cord into another knot at the end, which he pushed into the hole in the explosive at the base of the door.

He stood back and took a deep breath. It was cool, yet he was sweating. He had done good work. Triple redundancy; his instructors would be proud.

He took an even deeper breath outside on the kitchen's deck. He skipped down the steps to get a briefcase and small laptop out of the passenger side of his vehicle. Back at the wooden dining table, he opened the briefcase and ran his hand over the $100,000 in paper currency stacked neatly inside.

It's a shame to lose this, he thought. In fact, it made him sad. But the trap needed to be baited, and what was $100K compared to the $5 million he was going to make?

He turned the case so that it could easily be seen by the closest window and placed the laptop right next to it. Kinkade turned off the lantern and then opened that one drape enough for a peek. He grinned, walked over to the door, and checked the deadbolt one last time.

Kinkade drove up to the front of the house. He got out and walked up the five front stairs to look into the window on the porch. He needed to shine his penlight, but there it was: Perfect.

■ ■ ■

Gordan rolled his shoulders and tried to keep limber. He looked toward the roll-up truck door and thought he could make out a folding chair. He wondered if he should go down and get it so he could sit down, in case the men following wouldn't enter for a while or didn't come in at all.

No. It would be just his luck that they would enter just as he climbed down, foiling his hastily made trap.

He reached his long arms up to the steel beam that ran overhead. There were few men his height who would be able to reach it without jumping, as his arms were long. He smiled at the memory of a Captain who started calling him "Monk" in boot camp long ago.

He sure as hell wasn't going to ask what the hell the guy meant, but he wondered what kind of slang it was. Then he graduated and the Captain gave him a dimestore novel about a guy named "Doc Savage." The book was from the 1930s and an easy read. The main character was most likely the predecessor of Superman or Batman, possibly both. Turns out "Doc" had a sidekick called "Monk" that looked a lot like a gorilla, with long arms and heavy in the chest and shoulders. Seemed to Hudde to be a bit of a compliment, but he never could bend a penny between his thumb and forefinger as his namesake could.

Standing up this high, looking down, made him also recall his training at airborne school. He told people that he wasn't going to stop at being a Ranger. He had plans of getting into Delta or other Special Forces. They had a half-dozen SEALs in his class. They made a mockery of the physical training, sometimes even asking for extra PT when most others were bone tired. Gordan felt as if he could keep up with them but never said anything.

Beneath him, something made a noise. Gordan closed his eyes and took a deep breath. He felt the door open as much as he heard it. He knew it needed a big tug to get it to open.

It seemed like minutes before the door below him slowly opened. The first man leaned into the dark space. A singer on the radio from the back office belted out that he drank too much.

The first man below crouched and slowly walked forward, totally focused on what little light was coming from the back of the room. He was probably happy for the loud music.

The second man passed underneath him, and Gordan could make out the third form taking a step into his darkness. Gordan gripped the steel above him and swung out into space.

The first man had just reached the last shelving unit and got his first good glimpse of the small office. He stopped in his tracks and crouched. There seemed to be some movement, and he brought the gun level with his eyes.

Gordan dropped like a stone. He pulled up his feet to get as much momentum as possible as his knees landed on both sides of the guy's head. There was a *Crack!* as bones broke, and Gordan's 235 pounds stopped briefly before the man dropped, falling forward. Gordan rode the limp body toward the floor, doing a perfect parachute landing. He tucked his shoulder, rolled to get his feet beneath him, and then he launched from the floor at the second man. His fist came up from the ground in a "Superman" punch, his oversized fist a weapon of singular destruction, a sledgehammer on the end of a rocket. It struck slightly below the target's jaw line, cracking bone and sending a shock wave through the skull cavity.

The man stiffened like a board and fell back, making no attempt to brace for his descent. If the punch hadn't killed him, the fall onto the cool, gray concrete may have.

A small-caliber bullet snapped past Gordan's left ear. This was no time to duck or dodge, and he used his momentum to crash into the last man standing, driving his entire weight forward. The man was lighter and not ready for the impact. The final hitman staggered backwards, all the air in his lungs expelled by the impact of the heavier Hudde. Gordan grabbed his gun hand before the man was out of reach. He pulled hard down on the wrist and spun under the elbow, standing quickly to break it across his own shoulder.

He heard the gun land on the concrete — even through the scream of pain — and he pulled on the broken limb until he had pulled the man into a sleeper hold. The man went limp, but Gordan kept the pressure on for an extra thirty seconds to ensure that he was "out."

18

Lemme Dubois loosened his tie as he walked down the hall toward the master bedroom in the White House. Victor Crewbon had assured him of the future success of the plans they had worked on for so long. His arrival in Tehran — unannounced to any media — to sign a peace plan endorsed by nearly the entire Muslim world would shock and then impress the Christian world. The news would stress Israel, but only temporarily. Dubois believed the sheer weight of the prospect of a peaceful world would bring them around. Dubois did not believe that he had negotiated away too many of the positions that the prime minister had formerly demanded. He shrugged his shoulders, not really caring anyway.

He opened the door to find his wife already in her bed, watching TV. She turned down the volume.

"I don't understand why I can't come on this trip." Her eyebrows raised into a point above the frames of her glasses.

"Dear, I would be much happier to know you went on a shopping trip stateside or maybe worked on your afterschool programs. Besides, this trip is really Victor's baby. Without his contacts, it never would have happened. He has set the schedule for the entire trip."

"So he's going to get all the credit?" She couldn't help but smile. That would be unheard of.

Dubois continued to unbutton his shirt as he sat hard on her bed; he placed his right hand on her knee under the silky covers.

"Dear," he shook his head. "Without me, the entire idea would never have been put into operation. No one knows, and many would not approve of the tactics that we have employed to get to this point. Saturday, it will all become clear, and even the craziest of Republicans will not be able to vote against the final treaty when it gets to the floor."

He leaned back into her as he untucked the shirt and began to unbuckle his slacks. "In the glow of goodwill and positive press, I will begin to build a socialist platform that will survive any future president. I will get the votes necessary for it all to be legal, and I will use the constitution to destroy the constitution — one piece of legislation at a time." His eyes blazed as bright as his chemically enhanced smile. "Our names will not be forgotten, especially when I pull it all off peacefully."

"Oh, you haven't changed since I met you at Harvard." She reached up and rubbed his shoulders.

"Some dreams just don't die."

He lay there an extra few minutes before heading into the bathroom and retiring in his own bed. It was nice to feel her admiration again.

■ ■ ■

Bob awoke and found it difficult to focus his eyes. He was mashed nose to nose with Eddy. When he tried to pull his head back, Eddy's head came forward with his own. Something dark was wrapped around the two men's heads, keeping them in this position.

He tried to wiggle away, but he realized that he was lying side to side, secured to Eddy, and then pain shot up from his right elbow through his shoulder, reminding him that the American had broken his elbow and probably dislocated his shoulder.

A gray metal chair slammed down near the tops of their heads.

"Good morning, sunshine," Hudde said as he sat down, allowing his boot to rest on Bob's good shoulder.

"Or should I call you 'Bob'? Maybe you go by 'Bobby'?"

Hudde knelt at the grotesque form of two injured men cocooned on the floor. A black blade suddenly appeared right before Bob's face. A flick of the wrist, and the duct tape was sliced so that Bob was able to look up a bit easier.

"Let's review your new reality, Bobby. Let me tell you, I've even impressed myself with this little trap." He held up three IDs and shuffled through them "Um, I swooped down on Eddy there like an American eagle swooping in on a rabbit. I knew it was going to hurt, but I didn't dream it would do that much damage. I really think I broke his back in a couple of places. I mean, he's barely breathing."

Hudde stood and walked back into the darkness. It hurt Bob to try to lift his head to follow, so he allowed his face to press into the concrete floor and just listened.

"Now this guy — goat fucker here — looks like this is Danny." He whistled in a high-pitched tone: "My lord — *one punch*..." Hudde ran back to Bob's side. Bob visibly flinched, closing his eyes. "*Nobody* will ever believe me when I tell them that I killed a guy with *one punch*!"

Bob wanted to spit in Gordan Hudde's face, but he could not turn his head. Eddy let out a gurgle, and saliva mixed with blood slid down the side of his face.

Hudde took something from a side pocket and knelt again at Bob's head. He began to unfold a heavy plastic bag.

Hudde saw that Bob was watching. "Oh, this is just a heavy-duty plastic bag I thought I could find a purpose for."

When he finally got the plastic smoothed out and opened to its full size, Hudde set it down on Bob's shoulder.

"Listen, Bob. I find this so funny — we all know those aren't your real names. I've spent some time in Afghanistan, Bobby." He placed his right hand over his heart. "I know you fuckers are some dedicated and tough sons of bitches. I just got a jump on you because fighting on a mountainside is nothing like real spycraft — right?"

Hudde sat and straddled the two captives like a bull in the gates. He reached into his pocket and set something on the floor, off to the side, "Now, I apologize in advance that I do not have any cool drugs or even a facility to get you a little wet. I get the feeling that you are going to tell me that you'll never talk and all that, so let's get right down to it."

Hudde locked eyes with Bob and slipped the clear plastic bag over Eddy's head.

Eddy sputtered in the bag, and his legs, still taped to Bob, kicked as his body convulsed for lack of air.

Hudde kept the bag tight against Eddy's throat. He leaned into Bob and spoke through gritted teeth. "I'm guessing this is really the humane thing to do."

After several minutes, Hudde jumped off the corpse and Bob. He grabbed one of the four ankles and spun them around while he pulled a ball-peen hammer from the back of his belt.

He dropped the two men violently to the ground, following up with three blows to Bob's exposed left knee. The Norse god of thunder would have been proud.

The high-pitched wail from Bob almost shocked Hudde, but he jumped back on the two men, sitting directly on Bob's broken right arm.

"Now I know you won't be running off anywhere." The knife appeared in Hudde's right hand, and he reached down, cutting the tape from between Bob and Eddy all the way up from ankle to knee to chest. Then the black blade slipped past Bob's eyes.

Hudde raised the hammer high over his head, then smashed the hammer into Bob's left shoulder, eliciting another wail of pain before he pushed Bob's head against the concrete floor and raised his hammer high again.

"Wait!" Bob's eyes were wide. "Aren't you going to ask me anything?"

"You killed my friend and his family in Texas. What else do I need to know? I'm going to feed you and your friends to a pig farm when I'm done here." Hudde's knuckles cracked as he gripped the rubber handle, and he snarled his war face as he flexed to bring the killing blow.

Spittle flew from Bob's mouth. "My name is Haashir Muhammad Zafar."

Sparks flew from the concrete as the hammer struck the floor. Hudde dropped the hammer and put his hands around Zafar's throat. "What do I care?" He began to squeeze. Hudde roared, allowing his anger to escape through his lungs.

Zafar tried desperately to speak.

Hudde relaxed his grip.

Zafar's eyes were wild, open wide; spittle flew from his mouth. "You people have rules...I...I want a lawyer!"

Hudde laughed as manically as he could. Reaching over and picking the hammer back up, he smashed another blow down, breaking the collar bone of the prone captive.

The scream would have broken windows, if the building had any. Zafar took a deep breath. "I work for the *Mahdi*, our future Caliph." His breathing became ragged, and Hudde knew that adrenaline would now be helping Zafar and that more pain may cause him to lose consciousness.

"Fuck that shit." Hudde grabbed Zafar's throat and began to tighten his grip again.

"Victor Crewbon!" Zafar barely got the last name out before his air was once again cut off.

Hudde sat back onto the men allowing the hammer to rest behind his neck. A bulging bicep menaced the brutality yet to come.

"What would the President's closest friend and advisor have to do with any of this?"

"It is he who commands us; it is he who will remove the President's head."

Gordan fought the urge to yell, "*What!?*"

"Upon the prophet's grave, I swear this to be true. When the sign is broadcast across the world from Tehran, our soldiers within would begin our attack."

"Within where?" Gordan sneered.

"No swine."

"What?"

"Do not feed us to the swine you spoke of, and I will tell you." He rolled side to side, racked with pain.

"If this pans out, I swear it." Gordan set the hammer off to his left and stood.

Zafar no longer had the use of his arms or any strength to carry on the fight, and now his will drained from him. "Your President will lose his head on Muslim soil, and that will be the sign for our soldiers to begin." Gordan thought that he could see a slight smile on Zafar's face. "Many soldiers of Allah have crossed your borders over the last few years. We will destroy your oil refineries, poison the waters, derail trains, and kill your women and children. It is Allah's will; blessed be his name."

"Okay, I'll bite. When will this massacre begin?"

"I only know that it will be soon."

"So why the need to kill the SEAL, Jim Foster, and his family down in Texas?"

Zafar closed his eyes. "We didn't know about you, and it is not for me to question the *Mahdi*."

It was something that Gordan had expected, but hearing it firsthand made it all come true. He asked his next question for his phone, which was recording nearby.

"Victor Crewbon, the President's advisor, called you directly and told you to kill Jim Foster and his family in Texas, and then he told you to come to Washington — for what?"

"We were to find out what you know and whom you have told before we killed you and continued to the new war front."

Gordan lost all his energy; he exhaled deeply and looked up at the ceiling. He lost all his desire to fight. The government he was fighting for was currently and underhandedly making deals with the country's enemies, who were planning with the aid of another part of our own government to overthrow it. It hurt his head.

"Thank you, Zafar. I am a man of my word, and you will not be fed to the pigs."

Zafar looked at Gordan like he would kill him if only he could. Gordan dropped back onto his chest and squeezed the life out of the man, thinking of the small family in Texas while he did so.

He reached over and stopped the recording device on his phone, slipping it back into his jacket pocket.

After the violence, the bravado, and the killing, Gordan was sapped. He walked over with his small flashlight and found the interior lighting. There were no windows, so he switched on the large overhead lights to check for blood or any other signs that they had been here.

He picked up the small handgun and noticed that the gun had jammed. He thanked God that the gun did not chamber another round properly and also that this was all accomplished without any bloodshed.

A search of the bodies turned up the van keys, and Gordan went out into the night, now suddenly much cooler than it seemed just hours ago. He shivered from either the cold or the adrenaline dump. He found the vehicle parked on the opposite end of this row of businesses.

He put the bodies in the back of the van. Gordan tried to put everything back in the small parts stockroom where he had found them, and then he turned off the lights and drove the van to his townhome. He didn't relax until the garage door closed behind the van. He sat for a moment in the driver's seat, looking back at the three bodies. He ran a hand down his beard, contemplating the next move. Then he climbed into the back to inspect the steel footlocker there. It contained a couple of AK-47s and an assortment of Chinese grenades.

"You boys sure had a party planned."

Gordan grabbed a beer from the refrigerator and walked over to the cabinet that held his liquor. He took a shot of good bourbon before taking the beer into the shower. He allowed the hot water to cascade over his battle-worn body, and he sipped the beer.

*The **Famous But Incompetent** (FBI) would take him in and lock him down while they spent weeks investigating his claims. He'd probably do time for the deaths of the three Tangos.*

His phone rang from the top of the toilet, where he had set it down.

He twisted the shower control to "Off" and stepped out to answer.

"Go."

Terry Kinkade answered. "I was going to wait for morning, but I'm anxious to get this over with. I have a flight to catch late tomorrow night. Did I wake you?"

Gordan smiled. "Yeah. Lying here in my jammies, dreaming of what I could do with all that loot."

It was Kinkade's time to smile. "Good on you. You just keep thinking that way, and we'll all win." He cleared his throat. "Listen, I've upheld my promises. It's just that I think it best if we don't ever see each other again."

"Well, that doesn't exactly hurt my feelings." Gordan hoped to sound upbeat.

"So here is what I did. I found an old house that can't seem to sell, and I put the suitcase with the loot and a laptop with the account information right next to it on the kitchen table inside. You just need to walk in and pick it up. I'll consider our business over at that point."

"And just when I pull in, I'm guessing a shitload of suited fuck-sticks will take me down on some trumped-up charges. Am I close?"

Kinkade did not have to lie. "Not even close, my friend. You can drive around and look for those 'fuck-sticks' all you want and then drive up and peek in the front window. Your items are right there. Let me text you the address. It's near Joint Base Andrews. I was preparing my flight out later and thought it would be easy. Get your stuff, and then be gone. I suggest you don't delay. I've done my part. If some kids break into the abandoned home to drink on a Friday night, it won't be my problem if your suitcase goes missing."

Gordan wanted more info. "Wait — I have two things: First, shouldn't your team use me? I could make more money, and you know I'm good at what I do. Second, you must have some clue about where I should land when this is all over."

Kinkade chuckled. "I hated guys like you in the service — the jocks who got through physical stuff easily, the rah-rah flag-wavers who got everything handed to them. That's the beauty of this whole thing. I outsmarted every one of you cocksuckers. I don't give a damn where you end up. Fuck off, Gordan Hudde." He ended the call.

Hudde Googled the address and then fought the urge to go immediately. He knew he needed a couple hours of sleep, some breakfast, and then daylight to see things better.

He got his Remington 870 shotgun and slept with it nearby.

■ ■ ■

Terry Kinkade tossed and turned, trying to get to sleep. He was going to leave town with nothing but the news of an explosion to notify him of his success. But he now realized that he desperately wanted to watch Hudde walk through that ugly front door.

19

Hudde got out of bed and showered again just to wake up. He looked out the window with his first cup of coffee in hand and saw that some big, wet-looking snowflakes had begun to fall.

He jumped into his truck and started it. He allowed it to warm up while he looked in the crew cab for the snow brush, as the cold vehicle had begun to collect a few inches as it had sat overnight.

Gordan drove slowly in the Friday light after morning traffic. He did need to know if this entire Kinkade thing was bullshit or not, but he wasn't driving straight into an ambush. He'd been around too long for that.

■ ■ ■

Terry Kinkade did not know, but he had gotten a two-hour head start on Gordan Hudde. He packed some food and hot tea and made his way through the early traffic back to the carpet warehouse, a safe distance from his set trap.

Kinkade parked far enough away from the front doors of the place so as not to annoy the owner or manager, and he angled the

Cadillac just so that he could watch the driveway of the nearly empty home comfortably from his side window. It didn't matter when snow began to accumulate on the windshield, and he looked for a radio station where he could listen to the news of the day.

First Kinkade began to get chilled, because he didn't want anyone to see the exhaust on this now-frigid morning. Then he began to get restless. He moved the seat and did some isometric exercises, getting a bit warmer and then ultimately getting comfortable again, just before he realized that he needed to piss.

Kinkade looked around. He didn't want to use the business, and there was a bunch of trees just the other side of the building, a bit further down the access road he was facing.

"Fuck it!"

Kinkade jumped out and scrambled around his vehicle toward the trees. He leaned against one of the thicker trunks and began to relax as the steaming urine warmed what little snow had stuck to the ground.

He heard a vehicle but dared not move. The dark-blue pickup truck slid by, heading away from the house and down the access road. Kinkade knew that it was Hudde without even seeing him. When the truck was out of view from the soft turn and the tree line, Kinkade sprinted back and jumped back into his driver's seat. It still retained some of his body heat from his hours of surveillance.

Nearly fifteen minutes later, the same truck pulled into the same parking lot and stopped. The dark windows of both vehicles prevented anyone seeing into and identifying drivers. Kinkade cursed his decision to sit here. He slid down further into his seat and waited, feeling that, at any minute, Gordan Hudde would knock on his window.

■ ■ ■

Gordan pulled into some kind of carpet place and parked facing the house, just off to the Northwest about a half-mile or so. He turned off the truck and listened to the engine tick as it cooled rapidly in the cold late-morning air.

His binoculars gave away nothing.

He could see from this angle that the driveway went straight past the home and disappeared from view around the back; the roof of a barn or garage could be seen.

He knew that Suitland Parkway ran behind the house close by. But he could see only the guardrails if he scanned a bit further West where it appeared the small woods thinned. That was where the next closest home sat. Unless the home was filled with Tangos, there was no good location to stage an assault from.

He scanned this parking lot, and the one SUV and a couple of passenger cars were not enough to worry him. It was getting a bit warmer but still cold enough that most men would not be able to sit still, so Gordan sat back and waited.

It took about forty minutes before his desire to know outweighed his cautiousness. Gordan turned over the truck and inched out toward the driveway. He turned left onto the property and drove a hundred feet, or halfway, and then sat again.

Nobody gave away a position in the treeline in the back or came charging out at him, so the truck crept forward until he was even with the front porch. From here, he noted that only one set of curtains appeared to have a gap. Five wooden steps led up to the porch to a door painted a ghastly deep-purple hue. Maybe someone had allowed a child to pick out the color before they moved, or maybe it was even a prank of some kind.

He allowed the weight of the vehicle to pull it down around to the basement of the house. There was a padlock on the sliding garage door. Gordan checked the side door, and there was one there as well.

There was a porch off the kitchen in the back. Technically, that made it the second floor where he was standing, and a small balcony jutted out from the third floor; Gordan guessed that would be a master bedroom up there.

Gordan stepped carefully up to the porch and peered into the window that looked out from the sink. A bright yellow refrigerator stood guard just off to the side.

Gordan returned to the ground and walked back to the wood line. He could now easily hear the creek gurgle as the water picked its way under the overpass to find its way off to the coast. There was also some traffic noise from above as drivers had to push through some slush; there was no assault force gathered here.

Hudde continued around the trees and came up to the house opposite the driveway. He stood in the yard, looking out and down the access road. All quiet.

The yard must have been kept up a bit over the summer months, as the grass was not too long, but the trees had deposited many leaves over the fall, and they seemed to have been neglected as they congregated in wet piles. Nobody had walked through any of them or the snowy patches over the last few hours. If someone had, Gordan was sure that he would make out tracks.

He turned back toward the front porch, ran his leather gloves over his beard one time, and headed toward those rickety-looking five steps.

■ ■ ■

Terry Kinkade drew a deep breath and sat up after the truck pulled out of the parking lot and made its way up the driveway down the street. Each time the truck stopped, he would gasp and bitch under his breath.

"Come on, you overcautious bastard! Get on with it!"

But Gordan Hudde did not go any faster, and then he disappeared behind the house for thirty more minutes before coming up on foot around the opposite side of the home.

And then Hudde turned and stared right at him! Kinkade froze, the binoculars stuck to his eyes; he felt like he should wave or something. When the bastard began to move toward the porch, he let out a deep breath, but he did not allow those binoculars to move at all. He was determined to see the expression on Hudde's face.

"Oh, you stupid motherfucker! Those are all closed," he said as Hudde walked away from the door to try to look in the two windows on that side of the home. When he was foiled from looking inside, Hudde began walking toward that ugly door.

"Do it! Do it! Do it!" Kinkade chanted.

Hudde stopped and looked at the door but then turned and continued toward the other windows.

"Okay, have yourself a peek. See that tasty-looking cash just sitting there all alone?" Kinkade narrated.

Hudde placed his hands on either side of the window pane and leaned in.

"Yeah, there it is. You want it, don't you?" Kinkade jeered.

Hudde stopped and walked out to the rail at the front of the patio and looked out again, as if he could see Kinkade waiting.

"Come on, you pussy. You need that money."

Hudde turned and walked to the door, his hand stretched out from his body, heading toward the doorknob.

Kinkade wondered if he should have ear protection.

■ ■ ■

Gordan walked up each step gingerly. No need to break a leg falling through some rotted wooden stairs. But they held, and he stood before that comical door. Two windows to the left, two to the right. He turned to the right and tried each to see if there was a view inside. Nothing from either.

As he walked back toward the door, he almost reached out to grab the curved brass doorknob. But then he walked to the window he had seen from his truck. He knew the curtains appeared to be open a bit.

His breath fogged the window as his nose touched the glass. There it was, just like Kinkade had said—A briefcase next to a laptop. *The briefcase is probably filled with newspaper, or worse.* He pushed his face in different directions but could see nothing but those items sitting on an old, knotty-pine table and a few chairs. One was on its side, and Gordan couldn't make out if it was broken or had been left that way.

He turned and walked to the railing, looking out. His eyes were not focusing on anything, but his brain kept screaming at him — *They* were *trying to kill me.*

Could this possibly be real? Hudde pulled down on his beard before deciding there was just one way to find out, and he turned back toward the door to head inside.

20

This must be how small American children must feel as Christmas approaches, Victor Crewbon thought as he waited for the senior Special Secret Service Agent in Charge of POTUS, Donald Lippas. His men had probably handled the pesky Hudde character last night. He hadn't heard anything from Kinkade, so he guessed that the plan was still solid. Nothing could stop it at this point.

He was sure that Kinkade would be confused if Hudde didn't show up for whatever his plan was, but he would place his fortune on Kinkade just keeping the money and not saying anything. Crewbon knew what motivated Kinkade, and that was also a good reason for him to allow Kinkade to continue to work for him.

He could hear Marine One warming up outside.

There were two sharp raps to the wood outside his office, and then the square-jawed Lippas stepped in. "Sir, you wanted to see me? The President will be moving in a few minutes."

"I'm well aware, Agent. I wanted to let you know that after we return here from the United Nations this evening, Marine One will be heading out for some minor maintenance."

"Why wasn't I…?"

Crewbon interrupted. "Don't worry about this. We all will drive to Andrews in the morning. The weather is supposed to be terrible. Just a skeleton crew from here — do you have that, Agent?" He could see Lippas was about to interject. "We will take the 'tank' and one support vehicle to catch Air Force One at… what do you fellas say? Zero-dark hundred hours."

"Sir, with all due respect, that's not the way this works."

"Your protest is acknowledged, Agent, but, today, this is *exactly* how it works. You are dismissed."

■ ■ ■

Kinkade leaned forward. Any moment now.

■ ■ ■

Hudde had the doorknob in his oversized, black-gloved hand. He suddenly let go and stepped back. Something was not right. He walked down the same five stairs and headed around to the back of the home.

He looked up at the patio and walked up to look into the back door. He couldn't see much past the mustard-colored refrigerator. He looked up and could see through the slatted floor that the upper-floor sliding glass doors appeared to have no drapes covering them.

He leapt up, grasping the floor and corner post above him and, like a gymnast, flipped up and onto the floor of the top-floor balcony. He stood and turned to look at the view. He could see the traffic now flowing behind the house, and, when he turned back, he could see into a dark and empty room.

His knife easily sprung the latch, and he pushed the door open and gained access to the home. He slid the door closed behind him and stood still. If there were a double-cross coming, this is where it was going to be sprung from.

Fifteen minutes he stood still, listening to the noises from a hundred-year-old home and the beat of his own heart.

There was nothing in this room except an old headboard standing alone against a wall, left unable to perform its intended task.

There was a bathroom and another, totally empty, smaller room at this end of the hallway. Gordan walked to the opposite end of the hall and found another small bedroom with a hand-painted dresser, the same color as the door, with rainbow and unicorn stickers pasted all over it.

Obviously someone had talked a child into leaving it and starting over, or maybe a child had just outgrown the art form.

The drapes across the windows had enough of a gap in them that Gordan could look out. It was still. No cars screaming up the driveway.

Two more floors to sweep. Gordan crept as quietly as the wood would allow. He stopped cold at the bottom landing. Inside the front door was OD green from the layer of plastic explosives that covered it!

He swept the room with his eyes and then focused on the three triggering devices. They were all physical, which was a good thing. Nobody was going to activate it from a safe distance. Gordan reached out carefully and flipped the deadbolt to the door.

He turned slowly and walked lightly past the table with the briefcase and laptop sitting invitingly on it. He leaned into the kitchen and then looked out the window that looked out from over the sink. The back door was not rigged with any trap.

Gordan found the door that must lead down into the basement and began to slowly descend into the darkness below. He needed to clear the house before taking any other action.

■ ■ ■

Kinkade could not lean any more forward in his seat; the binoculars were pressing against the glass. His mouth hung open as Hudde's hand held the doorknob…and then Hudde turned and walked down the front steps and stood momentarily in the yard.

"No, no, no! What the fuck is wrong with you?" Kinkade slapped the steering wheel. "You saw it! You had to see it."

He threw the binoculars on the passenger seat and grabbed two handfuls of his own hair. "You paranoid cocksucker — just go in the fucking door!"

He wanted to get out and scream at Hudde as he watched him disappear down and around the back of the house.

Now what?

He began to rock back and forth as he tried to think about next actions. *Would he break in through the back door? Maybe he would check inside the garage first? I didn't rig any trap on the back doors — maybe that was a mistake, but I certainly had enough explosives. Then again, I could have rigged a simple cell phone detonator. But, no. Then I'd have had to stay and wait/watch, and, at first, I wasn't planning on staying.*

He took a sip of tea and tried to control his mind. His hands were shaking from the anger/frustration that was coursing through his veins like oxygen being carried by the bloodstream.

He lay back in the seat, closed his eyes, and tried to practice some breathing techniques. He didn't know how long he'd been sitting, trying to imagine a quiet place, when he bolted upright and screamed.

"Oh, no!"

At this very moment, Hudde may be inside, using the laptop to transfer the $5 million into his own account!

The engine roared to life, and Kinkade gunned it, heading straight from the parking lot across a small strip of dirt, mud, and snow before bouncing over a small gully and hitting his head on the roof.

"Aaaugh, motherfucker!" He nearly bounced out of the seat.

The tires spun briefly on the greasy pavement before he shot forward toward the driveway a half-mile away.

"I'm going to kill you!"

He tore into the muddy driveway and slid onto the lawn. The wheels kicked up mud and leaves as the vehicle slid as much sideways as forward. He nearly slid into one of the larger trees before the tires gained traction. He pointed the heavy SUV toward the wrong side of the house, dropping down and into the back yard before sliding to a stop near the garage.

He sprung from the vehicle's door before it stopped moving, running for the wooden steps. He pulled his Walther PPK from its holster with his right hand and kicked in the old kitchen door in one movement.

He ran straight to the wooden table in the front room. "Stay away from my money!"

■ ■ ■

Gordan looked for a light, but couldn't find one anywhere in the basement. There wasn't much on the dusty concrete floor — just a few boxes, forgotten or deemed unworthy of the move. What little light seeping in was from two small windows that appeared to be papered over with Christmas wrapping paper. Gordan reached out and pulled on a corner just as the roar of an engine could be heard.

Gordan pulled only a small strip of paper off the window and looked out just in time to see the black SUV sliding past his truck. Terry Kinkade, quicker than Gordan remembered, was out and running toward the stairs.

Gordan turned and bounded up the basement stairs, pulling his .45 from the small of his back at the same time he heard the kitchen-door frame splinter.

As Hudde came around the hallway to the front of the house, Kinkade was standing at the table, bellowing about money. Kinkade, coming to his senses, turned right into the left-handed punch that Hudde threw.

Kinkade dropped the small handgun and wobbled on spaghetti legs. He tried to reach out to the table for support, but his legs backed up without the rest of him. He fell across the chair that had been lying in the same spot for many years.

"Basheeshes," he said as he tried desperately to get back to his feet. He spat some blood on the floor when he tried to speak.

Hudde holstered his weapon and was on him before he could recover. Kinkade tried to throw a right hand, but it was swatted away by Hudde, who grabbed him by the jacket and yanked him to his feet.

Hudde righted the chair and slammed Kinkade unceremoniously down into it.

Hudde pointed at Kinkade. "Don't make me shoot you."

He walked over and picked up Kinkade's small handgun and set it on the table as he pulled up his own chair. Kinkade was seated with his elbows on the table, his head in his hands.

"I think my jaw is broken." He looked up and then leaned back, still holding his head.

"So that was 'your' money all along, huh?" Hudde nodded in the direction of the briefcase and laptop.

Kinkade was using both hands to feel under his ears where the jaw connects to the skull. "Yeah. I had a plan."

"So I imagine that, if I took a good look, the briefcase is full of some counterfeit cash," Hudde said softly.

Kinkade was rubbing his neck now. He leaned forward so that his elbows were once again on the table. "Jesus, I wish you would have just shot me. But, no. The cash is real. I figured that you would jump through the door once you saw it."

"If it makes you feel any better, I haven't dropped shooting you off the list yet." Hudde reached over and handled Kinkade's gun. "You think you're 007 now?" He chuckled.

"It's a good gun." Kinkade rolled his head slowly and began to work his jaw. "Okay. Back to negotiations. What do you want?"

"That's rich! *What do I want?* I want to make a deal and not have three goons try to kill me. I want to pick up my 'deal' and not get blown up!"

Kinkade squinted. "I don't know anything about the goons. Probably sent by some other friends you've made over the years."

Hudde sat silent and studied Kinkade. He could see that he was almost fully recovered from the blow, and he felt reasonably sure that he was telling the truth. He stood and walked over to the other side of the table. He didn't want Kinkade to grow a pair and decide to take them both out by dashing through the door.

Hudde reached into the briefcase and flipped through the bills with his gloved hand.

"Yeah, it does look real." He flipped open the laptop and hit the power button. "The account is real because you were going to take it, right?"

Kinkade nodded slowly.

Hudde continued as he set the Walther on the table to his right, away from Kinkade, and studied the screen.

"I guess you didn't need to leave me any instructions." He looked over to Kinkade and ran his right hand down his beard.

Kinkade walked him through the 'log in' to the Swiss account, and Hudde made the transfer before changing the password. "Well, that wasn't so bad, right?"

Hudde frowned. "Oh, don't be like that, Terrance. We still need to negotiate your worth so that I can get paid for letting you walk out of here."

Terry Kinkade gasped audibly. "They don't care about money, man. They're all wrapped up in other shit. Just name your price, and I'll do it." He held up his hand, asking for Hudde to slide the laptop across the table.

"Wait one minute." Hudde placed his right haunch onto the table. "Who is 'they,'" and why would 'they' not care about money?"

"Listen, Gordan. Dubois and Crewbon are 'big thinkers,' man, and they're both rich already. If you knew what I've done…" He looked up at Hudde quickly. "I mean what *Crewbon and I* have done, well, you wouldn't get it, I assure you."

Hudde reached over and picked up the Walther. "How about you humor me with the story? I got nowhere to go."

"Sure, sure." Kinkade pushed himself up, sitting straight, and Hudde could see he had gained his composure.

"Over the last two years, Crewbon has met and made deals with all kinds of 'bad guys' from terrorists, to dictators, to strong-man-presidents-for-life. I'm telling you, we even have most of the tinpot despots from half of Africa going along with this plan. I'm telling you, man." He held his arm out wide to show Hudde. "Almost the entire Middle East, as well as Russia and a few others that haven't really been helping in the 'war on terror,' if you know what I mean." Kinkade wiped his lips with the back of his hand. "I wonder if the water is running?"

"Keep fucking yakking." Hudde pointed the Walther at Kinkade to remind him why he was talking.

Kinkade nodded. "You name it — money, guns, drugs, even missile systems. We've wheeled and dealed across the globe."

Hudde scratched his chin through the heavy beard. "To what ends?"

"Come on!" Kinkade said, too loud. "I was their top security guy. I wasn't sitting in on their planning sessions."

"So you don't have a clue?" He raised the Walther a bit higher.

Kinkade threw his hands up, both palms facing out. "What do you care? One guy's not going to stop anything."

"The more dangerous their plan, maybe the more I'm worth to go get lost, right? Keep going."

"Okay, but, from here on, I'm just guessing. Everyone knows that Dubois is a fucking Communist, right? You had to know that. Maybe it's some big deal with Russia and China."

"So why the focus on the Middle East?"

Kinkade shook his head. "I don't know…maybe we fucked it up so much that they want us to fix it first. Maybe Dubois wants to force Israel into a peace deal by getting most of the world on board first? All I can tell you is that Crewbon is in tight with the Muslim tribes — *that* I can tell you. Somehow he's got them all on board."

"That doesn't bother you a little bit?"

"I'm needed for a while and very well compensated — so, no. What kind of pension does old Uncle Sam have for you?"

"Yeah, that's true. So what's this big secret trip?"

"Once they are 'feet wet,' nothing's going to stop their plan."

Hudde shrugged his shoulders.

"The first stop, and it will be brief, Tehran." Kinkade paused and enjoyed the shock that Hudde expressed. "Yes. They are going to sign this big deal and then go to Israel and see if they still want to play rough."

"That's fucking crazy." Hudde had kept up on the news. "The US president on Iranian soil? No, they'll just hold you all hostage. You're all fucking crazy!"

Kinkade started to stand, and Hudde leveled the handgun. Kinkade sat back down.

"No, that's what you can't understand. Crewbon is some kind of prophet or something. He's got it all worked out. I guarantee it."

"No, bullshit! I call bullshit; I don't believe they will take Air Force One to Iran." Hudde was shaking his head.

"Look, Gordan. I bet I could get you another $5 million if you just let me out of here. You'll see. Tonight, we leave Joint Force Andrews at 0200." Kinkade flipped his thumb at the window behind him. "They'll drive right behind this place when they head to Andrews."

Hudde now rubbed his own forehead. "So you're going to meet them at…" he shrugged his massive shoulders "…around midnight at the White House tonight?"

Kinkade shook his head. "No they're taking only the tank and one other vehicle. I'm meeting them at Air Force One. I can see it. You don't believe me."

Hudde felt as if his head was possibly lighter than Kinkade's at the moment.

Kinkade placed his hands palms up on the table and motioned "Come on" with his fingers. "Just slide that thing over, and I'll set you up." He looked up at Hudde expectantly.

The handgun was too small for Gordan's oversized hand. The Walther barked loud in the small room; Kinkade looked up in confusion as the spot on his shirt began to spread.

"Fuck you, Kinkade. You were trying to blow me the hell up only a half-hour ago." Hudde unloaded the entire clip.

Gordan threw the smoking gun into the lap of Kinkade's dead body and then sat down hard on the only other chair. It was his turn to sit with his head in his hands.

21

At Little Creek, Virginia, Navy SEAL Captain Jorge Hernandez was notified that he had a call waiting. He and his men were temporarily stateside for the funeral of fellow SEAL Jim Foster but now were planning their next duty assignment.

As soon as he put the phone to his ear, Hudde spoke. "Captain, this is Reaper. Have you been in contact with my superior?"

"Roger that." Hernandez leaned into the wall.

"If you and some men are up to it, America hangs in the balance —no BS. I'm talking the craziest shit you've ever heard."

"So, if it's that important let's go."

"How soon can you get to the Washington area, get some rooms, and then meet up with me?"

"A couple hours, but we ship out Sunday."

"That actually works out."

Then Hudde filled him on what he thought he may need and gave him the address where Kinkade was still reaching room temperature.

■ ■ ■

Hudde had a plan. It was spur of the moment and the only way he thought that the country could survive what he had uncovered. He hoped that he could convince the Captain that it was the right way to go, and then the mind of another experienced combat veteran could help look for problems with the hastily thought out plan.

First, he double-checked that the front door was locked. Then he headed out the back door, trying to make that appear secure even after Kinkade had destroyed the door jamb. He headed out to his truck to return to his townhome. He thought he could use his friends in the van.

The sun was high, but he didn't think anyone could point out where it was in the sky at the moment; it may as well have just set. The temperature had risen just above freezing during the late morning hours and now was dropping again. The area had seen snow switch to rain, and now snow was coming down again, slow and steady — and now it was beginning to accumulate. He was happy that it was after lunch and before the commute began again in earnest.

Hudde went inside his place to grab a meal replacement bar and another liter of water. He sat before his gun safe and began to transfer the $100,000 from the briefcase. He left the piece of paper with his new bank account information on the top of the stack.

Hudde had twelve years of savings and a 401(k). He hadn't checked recently, but he doubted he had more than $120,000 saved. He sat and stared at the potential before him to disappear. He had the training and know-how. *Why stay and put myself in jeopardy?*

He just couldn't find it in himself to back away. His love for the country that the founding fathers tried to make, that many of them lost everything to defend, made him set his jaw and head out to the garage. He would face this threat to the republic even if no one else would.

He switched vehicles so that his truck was in the garage, and then he headed out with the old white van. It took him several blocks to get used to how terrible it was in the snow and slush. He realized that the van probably was equipped with summer tires if it had come from Texas. He took the extra time to drive the side streets instead of getting on the expressway, where he didn't trust the drivability of the van.

He sighed a bit of relief when he pulled into the driveway of the place where he was supposed to have died. The van actually struggled to get up the low-grade hill to the house, wheels losing traction in the muddy, snowy, icy mess that was beginning to build. Hudde inched it over the top of the hill and then crept down and around to the back of the house, sliding every time he touched the brakes. He parked almost under the back patio.

He was thinking of waiting for darkness, but the location and the weather determined that he did not have to. He began dragging the bodies into the house.

■ ■ ■

"...The President of the United States, Lemme Dubois." The Deputy Speaker of the United Nations made a sweeping gesture to the President as Dubois took to the dais.

This was the reason that Victor Crewbon had selected young Lemme at college. Here was where Dubois felt most comfortable, and everyone always acknowledged what a gifted speaker he was. Today would be no different.

> *"Mr. Secretary General, fellow delegates, distinguished la-dies and gentlemen..."* he held out his arms to take in the entire room and the obvious TV audience, *"...and the entire world. I come today to discuss an issue that is*

as old as man himself; I will not walk softly over the issues
that have kept people from coming together, dividing us via
a line on a piece of paper. I will speak loud and passionately
about world borders."

There were some hisses from the crowd mixed into the applause.

"I hear that," he pointed into the crowd. *"And I will*
not spare my own country from a difficult topic. We, the
leaders of the great countries of the world argue today as if
these lines written on paper have been drawn there in stone
since the beginning of the world. Hogwash!" He slapped
the dais hard. *"I know you listen to the arguments we*
have here in America. We fight here screaming at each oth-
er as if these borders have never, and must never, change.
Americans must open their hearts as well as their minds.
Why, we started with just thirteen states and now, with the
recent addition of Puerto Rico, have expanded to fifty-one!"

He nodded to the applause.

"So I stand before you here in New York. You out there in
the world, and I say to my fellow Americans in Congress,
to the leaders in the Border States..." he paused, slowly
pointing up to the ceiling and then bringing his
hand down hard, *"Tear down that southern wall!"*

A roar came from the crowd. People began to stand and applaud.

"I cannot be president of a country that harasses, enslaves,
and, yes, sometimes tortures those trying to come to this coun-
try. To MY countrymen, I say this — they come only to

better themselves! Ours is a history of immigrants, and, I add, of good will. I will not allow the edicts of the former President to stand."

He paused now, waiting for some to retake their seats and to allow the thunderous applause to die down.

"We all must continue to strive for a One World attitude, where borders and nationalism do not interfere in the concept of justice! Who are we to deny anyone the chance for a safer, better life — a life where the government can ensure a safety net for each and every individual?"

He nodded and then pointed out into the crowd.

"I ask my friends in Poland not to be afraid and to allow a vote. See if your people really do want to fall back into the folds of mother Russia. I believe that they do, and that is where your fear lies. Maybe the feeling from the old wars is almost past; maybe we can have a European Union that includes nearly the entire continent! Imagine the progress that we could make then."

"To my friends in Israel, I say that the entire world sees what you are doing by 'expanding your security.'" He tilted his head, scoffing at the idea. *"Historically, we have been your closest ally, but today, even America must denounce your plans for your 'laser shield' technologies. We say, standing before the entire world, that you must cease this activity if you are to survive and thrive. I am compelled to tell you that every one of your neighbors have made formal complaints about your expansion of both offensive weapons and your border!*

"The world is changing for the better, and I call out to each and every one of you to join me in this new era of cooperation and singularity, a new era of understanding and fair shares for every individual!"

"Soon, I am betting that those you thought were the deepest of enemies will join hands as one community. Soon, the most shocking peace agreements in the last 100 years will come to pass, and then you will see the true intent of America and our deepest desires for world peace."

The applause followed Victor Crewbon as he exited the great hall. He wanted to snicker and rub his hands together. Lemme Dubois had just sealed his own fate. Nothing could stop his own plans now.

22

Captain Hernandez's four-wheel-drive pickup had no problems getting up the hill to the house. In fact, he stopped halfway up the driveway and looked up, waiting to see signs that Gordan Hudde was here. Only the rapidly disappearing ruts that the van had created proved that anyone had been here recently.

Hernandez stopped once again at the peak of the property, nearly perfectly at the side of the house. He took in the quick drop, down and around to the back of the home. He still could not see any other vehicle, but he continued down and around until he was parked between the garage and the white van. A black SUV sat off to the right-hand side of the garage.

Hudde was leaning into the back of the Cadillac's tailgate. He stood, turned, and acknowledged Hernandez with a thumbs-up.

Hernandez leaned forward and looked up at the deck above him. No one was up there, so he threw his truck into park and jumped out.

The two warriors bumped shoulders and then shook hands.

Hernandez nearly whispered, "Reaper. Good to see you, brother."

Hudde nodded, "You, too. Thanks for making the trip. Your guys safe out there and close by?"

Hernandez nodded. "Listen. The Deputy Director of the CIA calls and says a guy with your reputation needs some help with the Tangos who killed our brother." He paused, stepped back, and looked around. "You bet we come."

Hudde leaned back into the SUV and came out with an H&K UMP with four extended magazines in .45 caliber that he held up with a smile.

"Is that yours?"

"It is now." He turned and put the tailgate down.

"Let's get inside so I can give you the 'no-shitter' and then you can tell me that you are all in again." Hudde turned and started up the stairs. When he got to the back door, he turned back to Hernandez. "You better leave your gloves on. This is a crime scene. No sense in taking chances."

Hernandez pointed with his thumb over his shoulder in the general direction of the Caddy. "Does that mean we have company?"

"Nobody who's going to have anything to add." Hudde turned back, opened the door, and walked inside.

Hernandez followed, his head on swivel. He was trained to take everything in and not lose focus. He pulled his Glock .40 when he saw the shape of an individual in a chair at the head of the table.

"Don't mind him," Hudde said. He walked over and pushed a button on a battery-powered lantern sitting at the center of the table, holding down a map of DC.

"Oh, fuck. I know him!" Hernandez made sure not to step into any of the blood that had pooled under the chair as he leaned in and inspected Kinkade's face. "Guy's an asshole."

"Was an asshole," Hudde corrected.

"What the fuck, man?" Hernandez saw the other bodies lying inside the front room, now visible with the glowing lantern, and he walked slowly into the front room, following his gaze. "Christ — what the fuck is that!" He stopped a few feet short of the front door and inspected the configuration of the explosives.

Hudde walked up and put a hand on the Captain's shoulder. "Exactly why I stressed the back door. It's a long story, Captain, and we don't have much time."

Gordan began to unwind the story, from stumbling across Jim Foster to the dead Tangos lying just a few feet away.

"I knew Foster's report was full of errors or omissions. I never thought he was a good liar or poker player, for that matter. The report seemed devoid of any actual facts, and I couldn't figure out why the upper echelon didn't make him re-write it."

Hudde nodded. "Yeah. The White House was happy with the report, so the pentagon was, too."

"This is beyond difficult to believe." Hernandez paced to the kitchen and back.

Hudde pulled out his phone and set it on the table. "This will help." He played the confession from "Bob" that he had recorded in the parts facility.

"Christ Lord Almighty!" Hernandez placed his thumb and forefinger above his eyes and pressed as if he could push the thoughts from his head. "And Kinkade and Crewbon were front and center in all this?"

"Most likely, they gave the Taliban the location of your SEAL team, which got this...this tip of the iceberg...visible. I'm sorry I didn't record Kinkade; I know he would have shut down if I'd slapped the phone down in front of him."

"And you really believe that Crewbon intends to cut off Dubois's head and become the Caliph of this new Caliphate? I just don't know...I mean, why not just pass this along?"

Hudde looked at his phone. "We've got around six hours before Air Force One gets airborne. You believe anything or anyone will take me seriously and stop this trip? Dubois is complicit in this, even though he will be the unwitting victim in the end. It's his policies, his idea to reshape America — hell, reshape the world — that has allowed Crewbon to set this up."

Hernandez paced for another minute before stopping before Hudde. "I think you've gone mad..."

■ ■ ■

Marine One hit another pocket of arctic air and dropped twenty feet before the pilot could increase power to the rotors and level out.

President Dubois "white knuckled" on the edge of his seat through the drop and then leaned in close to Crewbon. "I knew the Israeli delegation would pull some kind of stunt!"

Crewbon smiled and nodded. "Tomorrow, they will rue the day. Trust me when I say that, after tomorrow, no one will ever remember that they walked out on your UN speech."

Dubois gave a "thumbs up" and leaned back, closing his eyes, trying to ignore the increasingly terrible weather.

Crewbon kept his eyes open; he looked at the spot where his blade would strike Dubois, and he tried to prepare his words for when he handed the head of the American President to the Ayatollah's outstretched hands in Tehran.

■ ■ ■

"…but I'm going to convince my men to help; I also see no other way to save the country." Hernandez held out his hand, and Hudde shook it earnestly.

"Then check this out." He pointed to the map. "We need to polish this plan up and get your men working on some of the other procurements ASAP."

23

Outside the White House at 0100, there was a three-vehicle motorcade waiting to take the President to Joint Force Andrews. A DC metro squad car was taking the place of the usual motorcycle Secret Service motor patrol, due to the terrible weather. Then came the President's "beast," followed by the Secret Service's own SUV; Agent Lippas and his best driver waited inside the President's limo.

Luggage and any equipment had long since been loaded onto the support aircraft already on the tarmac at Andrews. Two reporters, one print and one from a little-watched cable news network realized that they were the only two pool reporters who were going on this much-whispered-about trip.

They patted themselves on the back, and both plotted on how to make the President look great, no matter what happened on this trip. It was more important that they were selected on the next trip as well.

Their bags already inspected, they were shown to the back stairs to Air Force One and allowed to board.

Dubois waited at the door and put his arm around Crewbon as the two headed out into the cold, wet mess. It didn't matter to Dubois. He was jubilant at the potential success of his plan, he was hopeful that he would implement years of a Socialist rule right here in America. He grinned ear to ear just thinking about the history books that would tell of his rise to power.

"You have done it. The papers are already singing your praises for such bold action." Crewbon looked up into the face of the president.

"I was just trying to think of what the history books will say." Dubois squeezed Crewbon's shoulders.

Crewbon reached up and grabbed the President by the back of the neck — Dubois thought, *a bit too tightly.*

"I guarantee that you will be remembered long after your death!" Crewbon chuckled before letting go of Dubois's neck and stepping up and into the back of the "beast."

Agent Lippas turned from the front passenger seat. "Ready to go, Mr. President?"

Dubois nodded. "Let's go safe, but let's get going," and he pointed toward the front of the vehicle.

Agent Lippas keyed his microphone. "Let's roll." He turned to the agent driving. "Okay, Tommy, hit it."

Tommy leaned forward a bit and turned on the blue-and-white strobes before hitting the gas.

The agent driving the rear guard vehicle replied with one word: "Roger." The police officer hit his lights and replied, "10-4."

Lippas keyed his mic. "It's ugly out here, so nice and easy. I don't want to be plastered all over the morning news because one of us gets into a ditch."

Nobody answered.

As the three-vehicle parade slowly made its way southeast down Pennsylvania Avenue toward the 395, a man in a dark-green Jeep Cherokee reached over to his own mic and said, "Target moving." He made sure the open briefcase on his passenger seat was secure in its position. Inside the metal case sat a small black electronic device. Two antennae came up out of the back of the unit — one straight and about fifteen inches tall, the other corkscrewed up about eight inches.

Once moving, Lippas rolled up the security screen between the front and the President and Crewbon. He remained vigilant. He needed only to get the president to Andrews, and then he knew he could catch some much-needed sleep on the long flight.

Well behind the President's vehicle, the man in the green jeep keyed his mic again. "Confirmed southeast on 695. I say again southeast on 695 — over."

There were four distinct confirmations that came over the radio in response.

Agent Lippas looked at the face of the agent driving; it was intense. He could see the many minute second-by-second adjustments that he was making to keep the big vehicle riding between the lines. The snow coming at the windscreen, even at only 40 mph, looked like some kind of crazy white kaleidoscope.

Lippas smiled at the concentration and dedication of the junior man now driving. He reached over and flipped on some soft jazz on the radio. "Nice and smooth," he said to the driver. He was secretly very happy that they were not going to be on these roads for the morning. No way were the DC metro guys going to keep this road condition cleared up for the Saturday morning crowd.

In the back of the vehicle, Dubois was thinking out loud, waiting for a response from Crewbon.

"Seriously, why not form something like an American Union that would include the entire Americas?"

Crewbon shook his head and smiled. He wondered if Dubois was a bit light-headed from the business of the day.

"Lemme, I seriously doubt that Cuba would join anything. Think about it. Would you relinquish power if China or Russia came calling?"

Dubois was silent for a moment. "No, no, you're right; I wouldn't want that, either." He returned to staring out the window.

Nearly a mile behind them, the man in the jeep picked up his mic. "East on Suitland Parkway. Please confirm."

"Roger two."

"Roger three."

"Roger four."

"Roger five."

The jeep driver nodded his satisfaction.

There was no traffic with them, and only a few vehicles had gone by in the West lanes, opposite them. The slow-motion scene from a violently shaken snow globe played out.

The jeep driver keyed his mic. "Approaching point Alpha… in three, two, and one! Go, go, go!" He paused and then said, "Radio silence now!" He dropped his mic, reached into the case to his right, and flipped a switch on the small black box inside. A row of red lights came on across the front of the unit and began blinking in sequence from left to right. One by one, the lights all switched to green. His own radio began to emit white noise, and he turned if off.

Inside the "Beast," Agent Lippas got a lot of feedback in his earpiece. He turned down the volume and began to change frequencies, trying to silence the squelch.

"Holy shit!" The driver's eyes were wide, looking back over Lippas's shoulder. A Greyhound bus was barreling down the on-ramp way too fast for road conditions —hell, way too fast for *any* conditions.

Lippas reached over and touched the driver's shoulder. "Pick it up if you can."

If they were lucky, the bus would slide right behind them.

They were lucky, but not the following support vehicle. The bigger, heavier bus caught it perfectly, and both vehicles slid, as if they were one, toward the side of the parkway into — and then through — the guardrail there.

The armored support vehicle slid down the steep embankment, rolling over and over, and finally stopping upside down. The bus had stopped, the guardrail poking straight into the radiator like a sword through a chest plate. Hot liquids poured out onto the frozen ground, causing an odorous steam.

The bus driver climbed out of the damaged behemoth. He walked over and glanced at the black sedan, lying below on its roof, before looking back and waving at the green jeep.

The President's vehicle took more than two hundred feet to come to a complete stop. The metro police officer ignored the one-way traffic, as there was none at the moment. He drove up to the driver's-side window of the President's Limo. The officer rolled down his window and motioned for the agent to do the same.

"I'll go check," he yelled through the storm.

Lippas yelled, "Wait!" past his own driver, but it was too late. The police cruiser was already heading back to the wreck. Lippas had wanted to check on his communications equipment.

Captain Hernandez jumped out of the jeep and placed the communications jammer under the first seat of the bus. He came out to meet with the metro DC police officer as he climbed out of his squad car.

A Maryland State Police vehicle drove slowly past and then made a beeline for the President's vehicle. Lippas was now standing beside the "Beast," watching the trooper's car approach. It stopped alongside Lippas, and the window came down about four inches.

The driver yelled out over the winds, "Is that really the President?"

Lippas was looking back at the accident scene but nodded.

"I heard the call over the radio. Where are you headed? I'll get out in front."

Lippas nodded once again. "Good. Yeah — that's a good idea. We're just heading to Andrews." He covered his eyes from the stinging hail that was coming down now and turned back to climb into the comfort of the heavy vehicle.

"I got you." The trooper rolled up his window and inched out in front of the limo, the President once again moving in the right direction.

The metro police officer squinted into the storm. "This is fucking crazy," he said to the bus driver. "What the hell is wrong with you? Have you been drinking or something?"

The bus driver put his hand around his mouth to make sure his voice was heard over the wind. "No, not drinking…I did it on purpose." That's when the officer first realized that the driver was wearing a ski mask.

Hernandez reached around like he was placing the officer in a sleeper hold but really was placing a chloroformed rag across the officer's face.

The bus driver smiled through the mask. "Nighty-night, officer." He reached out and patted the police officer's hat, firmly seating it upon his head, albeit a bit askew, and then reached down to grab the officer's feet to help the Captain drag him up into the bus. Once inside, they handcuffed him to a rear seat before getting into the jeep and heading in the direction of Andrews as fast as they felt they could. Hernandez knew the Maryland Trooper would be taking his time.

The driver of the Maryland State Trooper's vehicle took off the Stetson and set it on top of his own communications jammer. Ahead, he could see bright-orange flares glowing out in front of a jackknifed tractor trailer. The truck was touching the guardrails at the far left of the three-lane highway while the trailer end pointed at the exit ramp ahead. The Maryland cruiser slowed down as the Master Sergeant was about to give a thumbs-up to the dark figure standing near the back of the trailer.

That lone figure raised an AK-47 and fired off two rounds that struck the back driver's-side window, shattering it and then the rear panel of the patrol vehicle.

The Master Sergeant turned the thumbs-up into a "bird" and spun out and down the off ramp.

"Jesus! Shot fired!" Lippas screamed into his radio; only gray feedback responded.

Lippas turned to his driver. "Step on it. No need to test the armor."

His driver, Tom, stepped on the gas, taking the right-hand turn to the off ramp, now just miles from Andrews. They could hear heavy rounds trying to punch holes in the steel, and the outer layer of "glass" splintered into spider webs as it stopped rounds from entering the cab.

Lippas put down the security screen. "Everyone okay back here?" He turned so that he could make eye contact.

"What the hell is going on, Agent?" Dubois was looking back and forth between windows. Each time a bullet struck the limo, he visibly flinched.

"Andrews is just down…"

"Holy shit!" Tom yelled out from the driver's seat, releasing the steering wheel so that his arms could cover his face.

24

Gordan Hudde sat in the big idling diesel dumptruck/sanding plow. The heat was insufficient, but the defroster was keeping the window relatively clear. Gordan guessed that the heavy load of sand in the back would help keep the big truck on line even in the worst weather. There were no streetlights here, and he kept the headlamps off and his foot off the brake to maintain light security.

He imagined that someone was getting an earful right now as they searched the Maryland Department of Transportation lot looking for his missing ride.

He turned over his left wrist to check the time and then cranked the window down to add his ears to his vigil. The wind was coming across the parkway above him, leaving him in a pocket of mostly still air on the access road, called "Woodland."

He was looking up and to the Northwest and thought he could see lights coming slowly. He put the big rig into gear and revved the engine. It broke free from the buildup of snow and ice that had begun to grow beneath the wheels and rolled forward. Hudde stomped down on the accelerator, and the rain caps on the exhaust danced.

Even through his engine noise, he heard the distinctive sound of an AK-47 firing, and he shifted once again as he neared 45 miles an hour. The Maryland Trooper's vehicle sped across his path, and Hudde ignored it, turning on all the rig's lights just before he struck the President's limo dead center as it, too, tried to cross his path.

■ ■ ■

Bright lights flooded the interior of the limo just seconds before they were struck dead center on the side. Metal screamed as well as someone in the back seat. The limo was pushed off the road and into a small ditch.

Lippas checked, and everyone was uninjured. They could not exit the vehicle from the driver's side, and a white phosphorus grenade suddenly dropped onto the hood of the large limo and began to burn through the hood.

"Okay, listen up." His head was on a swivel. "Once Tommy and I get out, we keep this wreck between us and the road and we head up to that house on the hill."

The two men slid out weapons pointed up, toward the empty cab of the truck, and behind them, in the direction of the parkway.

The President got out first, followed by Crewbon. Automatic gunfire sounded from somewhere above them, and bullets began to ricochet off the back of the truck and limo.

"Run from tree to tree," Lippas yelled at Dubois, pushing him forward. "Keep low!" He fired several rounds in the direction of the gunfire.

Lippas felt a bit of relief as he observed the Maryland cruiser drive back up, straight into the yard of the home. A dark figure could be seen as the driver stepped out of the car and placed his service rifle across the doorframe. The relief turned to terror as the shadowy figure began to fire in the direction of Dubois and Crewbon.

Lippas and Tom "leapfrogged" to the first large trees in the yard, trying to lay down fire to support the President and Crewbon, trying desperately to find some safety in the house above.

Somewhere, heavy rounds were fired, and Lippas felt ribs crack as .45 caliber bullets struck him just below and left of his heart. He stumbled backwards and yelled out as he fell, "I'm hit!"

Tom, not sure which side of the tree to hide behind, called out to Lippas. "Hang in there," and he fired two rounds at the truck lights as he thought he had seen movement. Then he turned back to the scrambling executives. "Run! Get into the house. See if they have a land line and call 911!"

Lippas tried to scramble to the next tree, and rounds dug up the snow in front of him. He decided that, if he was to die here, he would charge toward where it seemed the gunfire was coming from. But then, automatic gunfire rang out, and he curled into a ball and prayed for reinforcements.

Windows broke above them, and glass rained down. Dubois ran stooped the last 20 yards to the old wooden steps, where he squatted and called out to Crewbon, "Come on — we're almost there!"

Victor Crewbon was seated, leaning back on the old maple tree, thinking. How is it possible that all my plans could be shattered by a terrorist attack? He suddenly wanted to laugh. Then his own words came back to him. A *"terrorist attack?"*

He stood and leaned out from behind the tree trunk. He wasn't sure who he was yelling at, but he yelled out as loud as he could in Farsi. "I am the Caliph! Stop your attack!"

The Staff Sergeant with the machine gun was now standing at the back of the snow plow/dump truck, and he stepped up on the bumper so that he could see Gordan Hudde standing in the pile of sand in the back of the truck. "What was that?" he whispered.

Hudde shrugged and yelled back in Pashto: "We fight for Allah, who is great!" and he fired the remaining rounds in his magazine at the tree that Crewbon was hiding behind.

Tom took aim at the *jihadi* in the back of the truck and started to return fire.

Hudde, out of rounds, threw the UMP in the direction of the limo driver, jumped onto the burning hood of the limo and then to the ground, pulling his .45 pistol during the movement, and placed a round dead center in Tom's chest, knowing the Secret Service Agent's vest would protect him from death but not the impact.

Dubois took advantage of no rounds coming their way and charged to the ugly purple door, holding out his hand in the direction of Crewbon cowering behind the tree.

"Come on, Victor — run!"

Victor slipped. His shoes were not made for running in this wintery mess, but he managed to stumble forward and maintain an amount of momentum as he reached the stairs to the front porch. He took the first two steps and then fell forward, right at the feet of the President, slamming his face onto the wood.

Crewbon looked up, tears and blood dripping down his face. He sobbed, "Help me, Lemme," and he reached up with his left hand.

The President reached down and helped his oldest and most reliable friend to his feet.

"We're almost there!" He pushed down on the doorknob and leaned in.

The explosion lit up the night sky; Hudde fought the urge to duck and cover and moved to the dark-green jeep that had pulled up near the wreck. He briefly saw the fire in the sky in the reflection of the passenger-side window. Hudde nodded at the driver. "Captain," he said as he closed the door behind him.

The back doors slammed as the rest of the crew squeezed inside, and the jeep drifted off into the wintery mix without a word spoken by anyone.

25

In two days, the Vice President was sworn in.

After a week of mourning, the Senate hearing began. The congressional hearing started nearly a week later.

Gordan Hudde drifted behind the maintenance guy who was polishing up the new star in the wall of the lobby of the CIA headquarters. He guessed that there would be a small ceremony sometime soon.

Gordan handed his badge to the uniformed armed guard and then walked through the metal detector. It screamed in displeasure at the amount of metal he was carrying.

The guard nodded and handed back the badge. Hudde headed to see the Director.

Hudde waited impatiently for the large wood double doors to open. *Will this meeting require an attorney on my part?*

The doors opened, and Deputy Director Stevens blocked most of the light trying to escape the room. "Get in here," he said and turned, disappearing inside without waiting for a response.

Hudde stopped in the doorway. Director Smith was not inside the room.

Stevens pointed at one of the chairs. "Take a seat," he said, while staying standing near the front of the Director's desk.

Confused, Hudde sat down. His eyebrows arched high, silently asking the question.

"The new President wanted to make some changes." His grin was slowly spreading.

"No shit," Hudde nearly whispered.

"Not having a clue about a terrorist plan to kill the sitting President seems to be a terminating offense." Stevens sat down now, behind the desk.

He made eye contact again with Hudde. "The FBI and NSA are going through the same thing as we speak. You ready for a drink?"

Hudde realized his mouth was very dry, and he nodded.

"Make that two." Stevens nodded in the direction of the bookcase behind him. Hudde stood and walked over, sliding his hand over the shiny mahogany that held no liquor as far as he could see.

"Push on the third book from the right on the bottom shelf," Stevens said behind him.

Something clicked, and the bottom third of the second panel opened, exposing fine crystal and amber liquid.

"Sorry, no ice," Stevens said.

"Not a problem." Hudde poured two tumblers one-third full and carried them over, handing one to Stevens.

Stevens held his glass above his head. "Here's to being blissfully ignorant."

Hudde smiled, raising his own glass. "To never writing a report."

They downed the liquid and stared at each other, a quiet moment.

Stevens sat up straighter. "The FBI didn't find anything suspicious about Crewbon," he winked. "But we seem to be expelling quite a few people with Islamic ties in the last few days who had overstayed visas or made it across the border. I guess you won't find this story in any history books."

He sighed and took a deep breath so that he could continue.

"Kinkade got himself a star." He shook his head.

"Yeah. Your guys were just finishing up when I came through the lobby. He was a real hero; I'm sure the high-end hookers will be happy to hear about it. How are the Secret Service guys?"

Stevens nodded his head, side to side. "I visited them. They're pretty well shaken up, although their reputation got shot up way worse than they did."

Hudde shrugged his shoulders. "One's definitely better than the other."

Stevens reached into the center drawer and pulled out an envelope. "You want to talk about this now?"

Hudde sat all the way back and ran his hand down his beard. "I figured I could take a vacation where it's warm, sunny, has palm trees, and nobody shoots at you. If I get real lucky, I may see a pretty woman not covered from head to toe." He smiled through pursed lips.

Stevens shook his head. "You can do that without resigning. I'll put this in the safe for some other day." He threw it back into the drawer and slammed it closed.

"Thanks, boss." Hudde stood and began walking to the door.

"Gordan?" Stevens called after him.

Hudde turned.

Stevens pointed at Hudde. "We need you back, soldier, so take your time. But...you know...this is where you belong."

"I've not given it much thought. To be honest, this thing has been giving me some nightmares. I thought I knew who and what I've been fighting for. It seems the enemy made it in, not just through the door but to the seats of power." He stared hard at his boss to see his reaction.

"Not that last one," Stevens said, straight-faced.

Hudde's eyes narrowed; he grabbed his beard and pulled down. "The last what?"

Stevens leaned forward in his chair. "Thanks to you, they didn't make it through the last door. Think about what this place would look like without you."

Hudde nodded. "Yeah — there is that. See you around, Director." He turned, leaving Stevens wondering if he would.

Gordan Hudde will return in *An Angry Orange Sky*

WHAT IS BEING SAID ABOUT GORDAN HUDDE NOVELS?

A Deep Purple Hue

"With an extraordinary conspiracy story, this book is perfect for fans of *24*, as Hudde reminds me of a bearded Bauer. He doesn't always play by the rules and never bows to authority." — The Book Magnet.

"The perfect conspiracy, well-suited characters, a beginning that hooks you right away..." — Serious Reading.

An Angry Orange Sky

"With plenty of shocks and surprises, *An Angry Orange Sky* does not disappoint, and I have no doubt that we will be hearing a lot more from Gordan Hudde — at least, I certainly hope so!" — The Book Magnet.

"...Hudson expertly narrates what a single man driven by determination and courage can do to counter the evil forces around him." — Serious Reading.

"This violent, cinematic second entry in the Gordon Hudde Novel Series shows promise, with its surprisingly original plot, and despite a dauntingly large cast of characters..." — BookLife Prize in Fiction.

A Hint of Silver

"...Graphic and violent, the gritty manuscript powers along relentlessly... it's hard not to root for a hero like Hudde." — BookLife Prize in Fiction.

Words being used by other reviewers:

"Addictive, interesting, dark, disturbing, brutal, brooding, and exciting."

One reviewer said: "This novel would make a great movie!"

An Emerald Abyss

"...The flow and construction of conflict and character interactions are interesting...Former Staff Sergeant Gordon Hudde plays by his own rules" — The BookLife Prize in Fiction.

"This is a must-read for mystery lovers. It is well written and keeps you in suspense throughout." — Five Star Review.

A Retail Investigator

Many 5-star reviews!

"The book clearly outlines the excitement, risk, and exasperation that is part of the deal of being in the investigation business. The stories narrated are fun to read and extremely informative for anyone who is currently serving in or interested in anything related to the investigation industry." — Serious Reading.

Don't forget to leave your own review at the location you purchased this book!

Please come visit me at: http://www.
markhudsonofficialsite.com/

Or: https://www.facebook.com/
markhudsonauthor/

I can be found at Amazon, Barnes and
Noble, and other locations that sell eBooks
and paperbacks:

Smashwords: https://www.smashwords.
com/profile/view/sp4x2